Sixteen Small Deaths:

A Collection of Stories

Sixteen Small Deaths:

A Collection of Stories

Christopher J. Dwyer

PERFECT
EDGE
BOOKS

Winchester, UK
Washington, USA

First published by Perfect Edge Books, 2014
Perfect Edge Books is an imprint of John Hunt Publishing Ltd., Laurel House, Station Approach,
Alresford, Hants, SO24 9JH, UK
office1@jhpbooks.net
www.johnhuntpublishing.com
www.perfectedgebooks.com

For distributor details and how to order please visit the 'Ordering' section on our website.

Text copyright: Christopher J. Dwyer 2013

ISBN: 978 1 78099 684 4

A CIP catalogue record for this book is available from the British Library.

Design: Stuart Davies
www.stuartdaviesart.com

Printed in the USA by Edwards Brothers Malloy

We operate a distinctive and ethical publishing philosophy in all
areas of our business, from our global network of authors to
production and worldwide distribution.

CONTENTS

For Sarah and Amelia.

Crackle

Frosty speckles of rain pounce on the city streets and she leans into me with cyanide kisses and the faint glance of a dying angel. Time bursts into thirty-seven millimeters of broken ice, autumn wind whipping at my back with the force of a pipe bomb. She pulls me under the canopy of The December Club, frigid glow of neon lights the color of a summer sky.

"Let's go in," she says, eyes like sparkling green fireworks.

I shake my head, look to the moon for comfort. Four and a half years of bliss, crash love into a stone wall. Only a few more minutes with Molly, a few minutes for forever.

"Come on." I push the front door open and hold it for her, gentle waft of lavender spinning from the invisible halo above her head. She walks in front of me with confidence and the presumed attitude that for all of her life she's gotten everything she's ever wanted.

A Joy Division tune plays somewhere in the space between my eyes and the bar. Shudder of static, the melting quiver of lost time. Molly pinches my arm and smiles. "Don't worry," she says. "I'm the one who should be scared, not you."

#

I lick the edge of the shot glass, sweet traces of whiskey and fear. Molly's a few feet away, talking to the man who in a few minutes will change both of our lives forever. Molly's hands float in front of her chest when she talks, little blips of black fingernail-polish buzzing in the serene radiance of the bar like spider shadows. When she finally turns away from him my heart drops into my stomach. I'm afraid if I cough my insides will twist and convulse.

Molly walks over with a grin, eyes as bright as broken stars. "This is Kleyton Parker," she says. The man, short black hair and eyebrows like dead caterpillars, extends a hand. I ignore it and turn to the bartender. "Another one," I say, raising the empty glass to the air. The bartender nods and disappears.

Kleyton leans on the edge of the bar and sips a beer. He smiles when he finishes it and looks to the ceiling. He's cool and confident and there's nothing about him that I like.

"How many of these have you done, Kleyton?" I stand so close to him that I can smell the wispy edges of cheap aftershave.

He stares ahead, pupils following a buxom blonde entering the club. He drops a sawbuck on the bar and tilts his head. "Please, call me Kley. And, we only talk in the back." He points to a rusty metal door past the restrooms and kitchen. "Follow me."

We trail behind Kley, ruffled edges of an untucked dress shirt barely covering a brown leather belt. I haven't looked down but I can bet he's wearing cowboy boots. He holds the door open for Molly and I and darkness follows the eerie presence of silence in the rooms behind all is that wild and lively in the bar. Kley slams the door shut and it startles me. Molly twists her hair into a pony tail, little blonde stub poking from the throes of a frayed purple elastic. We're in what looks like a small makeshift office, two chairs planted in front of a card table. Kley plops down in the leather chair behind the table and invites us to sit down.

Molly sits first but it takes me a full minute to bend into the chair. Molly crosses her legs, slices of pale flesh peeking from the bottoms of her black jeans and above her little white socks. I sigh and before the memories of our life before today can cross my mind, Kley's voice cuts through the momentary fog. He tosses his legs up on the side of the table, collected and calm in the face of something I'd never thought Molly would ever do.

"I trust you brought the rest of the fee." Kley nods at Molly, who produces a small manila envelope from her purse.

"Two thousand," she says. "It's all there."

"Great." He looks at me for a moment and smiles. "Cheer up, cowboy. She's about to experience something that most people can only dream of."

"Yeah." I have nothing to say but my heart flutters for a single second, blood sloshing and dancing and fearful of every beautiful moment I've spent with the woman next to me.

"Two rules," Kley says, looking at us with red cheeks and serious eyes. "First, no moving or helping or touching her. I'm in charge and no matter how much blood or screaming I need you both to sit still and be as calm as possible."

"Fine." Molly arches her back, something she does when she's nervous. "And the second?"

Kley stands up. "There are no refunds."

#

I sit in the corner of the room, sweaty thumbs wrestling each other as Kley engulfs Molly's wrists in aged black leather straps to the rusty metal chair in the center of the black-and-white tiled floor. He steps away to a rolling desk tray that's lined with metallic instruments. He slides on a pair of purple latex gloves and sighs, eyes closed and hands pressed together.

Kley looks in my direction as he makes his way to the surgical tray. "Remember what I said," he says, pointing at me with a purple finger. "Especially you, muchacho."

I nod. Vision fades in and out, single light bulb swaying in a momentary graceful breeze. Kley's shadow swoops over Molly's figure and I can only imagine what she's thinking right now. Kley chooses a slender blade from the tray, plastic fingers clenching its black wooden handle.

He wastes no time. The opening hack happens in slow motion and when the first crimson drop hits the tuxedo-colored floor I have to turn away. Molly lets out an apocalyptic scream and it's then that I can see her face. Eyes glossed over like two wet marbles, mouth agape and cherry lips glistening in the pale synthetic light. I know she can see something because the next

3

swipe of the blade elicits nothing but her dead hand careening toward the tile without a single shout.

She sees it. She sees beyond the brick wall, beyond the pain and beyond everything we ever knew.

Kley unhinges the shackles and places a navy blue towel around the fresh stump. What's surprising is the lack of panic on his face. At this point I jump forward and Kley catches me.

"No," he says. "We'll take care of it." He fishes his cell phone out of his front jeans pocket and says a few words after dialing. Within a minute or two a husky figure enters the room and slugs Molly over his shoulders.

Kley pats me on the back. "This is why I do this. She knows what she saw." He tosses the phone next to the surgical tools. "Follow Hank, now. He'll drop you guys off at the hospital."

#

I sit and wait for her to wake up. Even with scraggly hair and a bloody patch where her right hand used to be, she's gorgeous. I slip my fingers into hers and she opens her eyes. She stares straight ahead for a second before taking a deep breath.

"Baby," she says, lips dry and cracked. "There's more... more..."

"What do you mean?"

She pushes away my hand and points to the window, slow crawl of sunlight peeking into the hospital room. Molly sits up, lips now careening into a powerful frown. "We're not alone. They're all over the place. Look..." The black tip of a fingernail cuts the air between us and the window. "I saw it, baby. I saw *them*."

Goosebumps march up through the skin of my hands and down into the marrow. Molly turns to me and the first thing I notice is that one of her once-green eyes is now a dark shade of gray.

#

I open the front door to our apartment and let Molly in ahead of me. She's quiet and walks slowly. She says the stump doesn't bother her. She spent two nights in the hospital and only did she sleep on the car ride back home. She won't talk anymore about what she saw, what she felt. I drop her duffel bag in the corner of the living room and head into the kitchen. She's sitting at the edge of the table, one hand clenched into a fist. Burgundy mascara slithers down her cheeks in a mess of tears and curls under her chin without hitting the table.

I sit in front of her. "What's wrong?"

She looks away and stares out the kitchen window. "They're here, baby. They're all over the place."

"Who?"

"They want you to see, too. They want you to be enlightened."

"Molly, you have to tell me who *they* are. Please."

She leans in and pecks a quick kiss on my cheek. She whispers at first, and when she tells me everything I need to know, I sit back and wonder how long it'll be before I can schedule an appointment with Kley.

#

I dial Kley's number and he picks up on the third ring. I can't believe what I'm asking of him and never in a million dark years would I need to feel the type of pain Molly experienced only a short few days ago.

#

"Your gal didn't come with you?" Kley snaps the bottom of the latex glove and my heart jumps through my ribcage.

"No."

"Well, that's just dandy." He begins to strap me into the chair but I shrug his efforts away.

"Don't need to do that. I'm ready."

Kley nods and pulls one of the blades from the tray. He holds it to the light, insipid refraction of light and ash. He traces the edge of his finger alongside my left wrist and I recoil out of excitement and fright. He brings the blade to the sky and comes down in a quick slice. White hot flash of pain funnels from the tip of my toes and tings the middle of my bones. By the time it reaches my brain I can see it. Their eyes, quick red slivers of glowing light, like fleeting bursts of comet dust. Slender appendages and crooked smiles, oval skulls and a skeleton allure. Another hack and the world stops spinning. Their mercurial motions, both fast and slow. Leaden skin and eyes of fire, they're all around us.

I can see them.

December

I could almost see the heartbreak in my stepfather's face, the way the morning sunlight would quickly dissipate and leave only the natural cobalt blue of his old and tired eyes. It was like I just told him that his nearly twenty-two years of raising a boy that wasn't of his own blood was a waste of time. Twenty-two years of a union laborer's life, money and sanity spent watching a disheveled child bloom into what he would at one point call a 'man.'

"Not a single word from him in over two decades," he said, "and now you're ready to drive five and a half hours to see him like he had only gone out for milk during that time."

I shook my head and placed a hand on his shoulder. "Listen, Dad. Even though I can't remember the time when he was around, I feel like I owe it to him to at least sit for a while with a cup of coffee, let him know about all the *good* things in my life that he's missed."

He sighed and turned away. "Trevor, all of my life I've given you nothing but the honest insides of my heart. I don't understand how you could so eagerly embrace a man, a so-called 'father,' that *abandoned* you and your mother when you were just a child."

"Dad…" I looked inside but couldn't find a thing to say that justified the small overnight bag that was sitting so gently in the backseat of my truck. The truth was that all of that anger and rage had disappeared years ago when I realized it didn't matter if the man that raised me was my natural father or not. What mattered was the countless hours teaching me how to ride a bike, the days and days spent in the little league baseball park. What I would always remember were the nights in the local drive-in, the early Saturday mornings fishing when the first light of day would rise above the darkened rim of the horizon.

"You're old enough now to do whatever you want," he said, nose crinkled into the typical Gregory J. Armstrong sneer that I feared whenever I came home from school with a horrid report card or a broken bone from playing football with the neighborhood kids.

"Dad, I can understand why you're upset, but please just listen to me for a minute." I sat down on the edge of the kitchen windowsill and pulled out a chair from under the table. "Just sit with me for a minute, please."

The sneer dissolved into wrinkly cheeks and eyes of winter. He sat down with a deep and resounding breath, arms crossed as if ready to deal with a used car salesman. "You have five minutes before I start dinner."

I smiled and nodded. "This trip is more out of curiosity than anything else, Dad. Believe me, there is nothing that this man is going to say that's going to ever make me smile like you make me do. I know what he did to Mom and me, and there's no room in my heart left for someone that abandoned their only child without an explanation. You are my father, biological or not, and nothing is ever going to change that." I was always afraid to cry in front of him, and this was no exception. I could feel my eyes water with the residue of a million memories. "I'm going to take a ride and have a cup of coffee, maybe stay a night at hotel nearby if the weather's too bad to drive. I'm going to get closure from him, and then I'm done with this small chapter of my life."

My father pinched the end of the kitchen table, crumbling aged pieces of maroon paint between his fingertips. After a minute or two he stood up and looked out the window. The beginnings of snow fell from the December sky, day beginning its descent into the darkness of night. He pushed the chair back and leaned against the edge of the table. "I'm not angry that you're going, Trevor. I'm angry that he even had the nerve to call you. The minute he walked out on you and your mother was the minute he lost out on watching you grow up." He cleared his throat and pulled open the kitchen curtains, his eyes darting back and forth between the waves of plush white snow sticking to the oak trees outside of the house. "Just remember where your home is. I know you don't live here anymore, but this house is where your heart is. No matter what this man says to you, that's the only thing I want you to remember, Trevor."

My lips curled into warmth. "I promise, Dad."

"Good. And I want you to think of your mother when you see him. She may not be with us anymore, but I know she's thinking the same things that I have ever since he called you."

I nodded in agreement.

"You're staying for dinner, I hope. Nothing better on an early winter's evening than a hot bowl of chili." He was already standing next to the refrigerator, pulling out a fresh package of ground beef. "Feel free to give me a hand over here."

"I'd love to, Dad."

#

I woke up around eleven-thirty. My father had thrown a red-and-black patchwork quilt over the lower half of my body. We ended up talking for hours after dinner, which led to a round of cards and too many glasses of wine. I told him I wanted to rest my eyes a bit on the couch before taking off for my apartment. Before long, the mix of wine, chili and smiles dragged my body into a satisfying fit of slumber.

I sat up on the couch and for a moment I was a teenager again, the inkling of inebriation still a hazy fog in my youthful mind. The couch was much older than me, made of fluffy cushions and plush velvet lining. I would routinely fall asleep in the living room since there was never a television in my bedroom. Even after I left for college, the best night's sleep came with a little alcohol and a weary body resting on an aged three-cushion sofa.

My father shuffled about in his room a floor above. He was

always a restless sleeper, victim to overexcited legs that needed a quick lap or two around the room before falling back to weariness. I didn't want to disturb him so late at night so I instead walked into the kitchen for a glass of water. Cool liquid slid down a parched tongue and the fuzzy siren-call of sleep was nipping at the back of my head again. I paused and peered out the kitchen window before heading back into the living room. A perfect coverlet of snow dressed the front yard, great oak and pine trees now housing a winter's dose of frozen ice.

I laid my head under a quilted throw-pillow and remembered one of the first moments I realized my stepfather loved me like I was his own. It was only a year into he and my mother's marriage, and I spent the majority of my time wondering where my real father had retreated after ditching what I imagined to be the two people closest to him. It was the early winter and the multi-colored fireflies of Christmas lights adorned the trees in our front yard. I sat on the front steps, watching a layer of thick snow dance amidst a perfect winter landscape. Crushing a fistful of snow and ice in my hand, I tossed it as far as I could manage. It smacked the end of the driveway in a soundless explosion. My stepfather emerged from the front door, wooly jacket covering his hairy and tattooed arms. He sat next to me and smiled, scraping snow from the stairs with his boots.

"Has anyone ever shown you how to make the perfect snowball?" he asked.

I shook my head, staring at the ground.

He leaned forward and scooped a mix of slush and puffy snow, curling it in his fist like it was a hardboiled egg. I watched as he pouted his lips and worked the ice until it was nearly perfect in circumference. He showed it to me, holding it between the tips of his now red fingertips.

"This," he said, "is good enough to throw."

He tossed it with a gentle heave, nearly tripling the distance of my throw a few minutes earlier. It shattered with a glittery boom, fractures of moonlight shining with each mirrored piece.

I sighed and adjusted the pillow under my head. I could see the reflection of the storm's final drippings on the blank television screen a few feet away. The shuffling upstairs stopped, and I silently wondered if my father was going to experience the same memory-laden dreams as I was about to encounter.

#

The aromatic pleasure of fresh coffee woke me from a solid dreaming state. I could hear spoons and pans colliding in the kitchen like a momentary morning symphony. I lifted my legs off the couch and stretched the stiffness in my back. Before I could stand up, my father greeted me with a smile and a cornflower-blue mug, wisps of steam floating from its open mouth.

He sat next to me and placed the mug on the wooden coffee table a few inches away. "Just the way you like it," he said. "A little bit of skim milk and three spoons of sugar."

I took a long sip, sizzling springs of caffeine jolting my body into full consciousness. I crossed my legs over the table and pointed behind me. "How does it look out there?"

My father inched his head over his shoulder and peeked out the living-room window. "Shouldn't be too bad out there, son. I bet all of the main roads and highways should be fine." He cleared his throat. "What time do you have to meet him?"

"Noon, or a little after."

My father nodded, then stood up. "Well, you're going to have to get some eggs and toast in that body if you want energy for that long drive. It'll be ready in a few minutes."

"Great. Thanks, Dad." I tilted my mug towards him in a joyous toast.

He chuckled. "Save the theatrics for breakfast."

#

I shoved my hands through my jet-black pea coat and silently wished for summer. When I was a kid, my father and I traveled to a bakery outside of town for a cake for my mother's birthday. The roads were icy, and one quick turn forced our Jeep into a nearby tree. Neither of us was hurt, but since then I've been afraid to drive with snow and ice on the road.

I was about to open the front door when I heard his voice from behind me.

"Trevor?" My father stood with a silver travel mug in his arms. "I know you're not going to forget our discussion last night, but please, do not let this man sway you with anything, not even memories of your childhood. Your mother swore that she would never let him see you again."

I blew a round of cool air through my teeth. "Do you think I'm breaking Mom's heart by going through with this?"

"Not at all," he said, tightening the cap on the mug. "If she were still alive, I know she'd give you her blessing to see him because you're old enough to deal with that chapter of your life." He handed the mug to me. "Here, some coffee for the road. I'll feel better if you call me when you get there."

"I'll ring you as soon as I pull up to his house."

"Sounds good." He initiated a hug that could have lasted for an hour. All I know is that it felt like I was a kid again; the gentle push of his muscles against mine was not nearly as strong as it was years ago. I found myself pressing my forehead into his shoulder, something I would do whenever I was nervous.

"It'll be okay," he said, letting me go. "Now, go on. There's a long drive ahead of you." He reached into the back pocket of his jeans and pulled out a small envelope. "Wait...I wanted to give you this," he said, shoving the small beige envelope into the inside pocket of my jacket. "If you feel that this encounter is going to stir up unwanted emotions, open that little envelope and I promise that it'll bring a smile to your face."

"Thanks, Dad."

We said our goodbyes and in minutes I was behind the wheel of my car, engine beginning to purr in the shriveled air of another winter's day.

#

The conversation last week only lasted a few minutes. My cell phone rang with a number I had never seen before. The voice on the other line sounded familiar, but I didn't know who the caller was until he said my name with a long and extended breath. For the first minute, every muscle in my body quivered with an icy chill. When you think someone is long dead and forgotten and all of a sudden their voice is loud and clear on the other line of the telephone, you forget where and who you are. You forget that time has passed. You forget that this man on the other line made the decision to cut you out of his life over two decades ago.

You forget that he's just an outsider now, nothing more.

I don't know why I agreed to meet him, but I said "Yes" after thirty seconds of hesitation. I canceled two days of consulting projects with my clients and packed a small bag, eager to spend the night before the meeting with the man who actually raised me as a boy.

Five hours after setting out on Interstate-95 and I was idling two houses down from his. I shut off the truck and leaned my head against the seat. My eyes closed, I imagined what he looked like now. I hadn't seen a picture of him since I was a teenager, and I couldn't even remember if we shared the same eye color. I couldn't remember what his favorite food was, what he liked to do on a winter day. When I swung my hand on the door handle, the cold tinge of metallic touch reminded me why this man wasn't a part of my life anymore. I refrained from opening the door, hoping that I would summon the courage to leave the truck and knock on his door in just a few seconds. A few seconds turned into a few minutes turned into a few tears.

I didn't picture a person hopelessly wondering if his son grew up to be a man. I didn't picture a person spending their days hoping that one day his son would just walk right back into his life as if nothing had occurred oh so many years ago.

An hour burned off the truck radio and it was at this moment when I pulled out the envelope my father had shoved into my pocket, the one I now realized was dressed with the purple cursive handwriting of my mother. I flicked open the top and a single picture fell onto my lap. My mother's eyes were the first thing that came to me. Two drops of perfect green, the color of an uncut pine tree glimmering in the morning sun. Snowflakes were frozen in the air and the three of us were smiling as if we knew that life would give us nothing but the best. My father had one arm draped over my mother's shoulder, the other barely pinching my cheek. I couldn't quite recall when the picture was taken, but I knew that this was a sliver of happiness, a flash in time where nothing else mattered except the love burning between these three souls.

I turned on the ignition and blew past his house, not taking a second to see if he was standing by a window. Eyes focused on the road, and soon enough I was flying on the highway, eager traces of snow falling from the sky like little rogue angels dancing in a winter solstice.

#

I found a hotel less than an hour later. I plunked down my credit card at the front desk and asked for the cheapest room they had available. I knew that I wanted to sleep off the day, let the thoughts in my head burn into embers wild as a forest fire. Two flights of stairs and my room was in the very corner of the floor. I didn't bother to turn on the television, just kicked off my boots and placed my cell phone on the nightstand next to the clock radio.

At some point, my eyes closed and I remember the cooling whispers of the night beckoning me to slumber.

#

My cell phone rang around three in the morning. On the second ring I jerked out of a dead sleep, unaware I was resting on a hotel bed. I flipped open the phone without ever seeing who the caller was. The voice was a woman's, and if I didn't know that I was now fully awake I would forever swear that what she said was just the soundtrack to a temporary nightmare.

Her name was Rianna Peterson and she was a doctor calling from Massachusetts General Hospital. My father had dialed 911 and only a second after the operator answered, silence spilled from the other line. Police and an ambulance rushed to the house and found my father crumpled on the kitchen floor, his fingers still touching the receiver. He had experienced a massive heart attack shortly after noontime. Doctor Peterson said the paramedics found him dead.

I closed the phone and immediately leaned forward, ignoring the urge to let my insides spill to the carpeted hotel floor.

#

I drove that night with fire in my eyes, the smoldering strands of shock still waltzing in my head. The ride to the hospital should have taken three hours, but with my foot on the gas and my heart in my hand, I walked through the front doors in just over two. I was barely coherent at the front desk, managing to say the words "father" and "Armstrong" and "heart attack."

Doctor Peterson greeted me a minute after, olive skin somewhat comforting in a sea of lost souls scattered about the hospital lobby. She shook my hand with the grace of a beautiful woman and asked me if I was okay. I told her "No" and smiled, unaware that I was gazing into the distance.

"I know this is difficult for you, so I'd be happy to call any relatives that might need to know what happened." She placed a hand on the side of my arm, unpainted fingernails plucking the rogue fuzz from my jacket.

"Yeah," I said. "His brother, my Uncle Charlie. If you can, please call him." I shook her hand again and walked away, forgetting to button up my coat as I walked out the front doors and into the throes of December.

A gentle sniff of the air told me that another storm was coming. There were already four inches of snow on the ground, and before long I'd be wondering when winter would be over. I knelt down and ran my fingers along the concrete, swirling figures into the ground that were symbolic of my confusion. I stared out into the night, half moon poised in the sky like a low-hanging slice of glowing frost. I removed my gloves and shoved them into my pocket, letting the back of my boots support my backside as I knelt down to scrape up a handful of dirty ice and snow.

I packed it into a ball, watching the flesh of my fingers begin to flush with red. Smile upon my face, I closed my eyes while I worked the snow until it was as hard as baseball. I opened my eyes and held it in the night air.

It was good enough to throw.

Sometimes You Can't Wait Forever

She exhales a strand of icy vanilla lace and my heart freezes with uncertainty. The beeps and whirls of the ventilator are a dazzling lullaby and my eyelids start to drop and barely open again before her hand squeezes mine. I've spent fourteen straight nights in this room with her and at least once a day she'll grasp my hand and give it the lightest press. The doctors say it isn't a sign of things to come but I spoon hope into my mouth everyday regardless of the world raging outside of my head.

Filthy orange moon in the evening sky and before long I'll drift off into another fit of slumber without her gentle embrace. I squirm into the cot next to the bed and hear the creaking of its rubber ends against the sterile hospital floor. The nurses in the intensive-care unit walk past the room and each one looks like they're afraid to smile.

Autumn's chest heaves in and out with the help of a machine. I can remember nights watching her sleep before the accident, watching the beautiful chasm between her breasts lift in a strand of moonlight as my breaths drew long and comforting. She wears a white gown with jade polka dots and for only a moment is she the most gorgeous being in this building.

I clutch her hand in mine and run a finger along her nails, bits of crimson nail-polish like a map to her past. She painted them only a few hours before nearly dying and I hope that I never see the full pink under her fingernails again.

My eyelids grow heavy and the siren of sleep creeps into my veins, body tired but my mind running with a hundred uneven memories. I stare at the array of stars just beyond the window until I can't feel my arms or legs but only the dry touch of Autumn's skin.

#

Dead tree limbs dress a perfect mirror of ice and snow, azure sky painted above the horizon. Sparkles of freezing water drip onto my face and the landscape smells like a mix of bourbon vanilla and saffron. Vision is hazy and circles of white light adorn the film reel in my mind, stains and burns of an unforgiving world given to the throes of December. I take a step forward expecting to fall through a thin layer of ice but my steps are weightless burdens on its fragile frame.

Autumn's bright red hair speeds by like a flaming comet and I don't realize I'm smiling. Her arms are wrapped around me and her breath escapes from cobalt lips, tiny clouds of white dissipating before the glitter of winter touches my face. She's talking in slow motion and I struggle to decipher the words. Her eyes are as blue as a serene ocean and my heart flutters with the recollections of our life together. She brings a red fingernail to my nose, lets it slide down to my upper lip. Autumn leans in for a kiss and my lungs fill with chilled love. It feels like I haven't kissed her in forever and I want to hold on to this moment until I'm buried with her in the frozen ground beneath our feet.

Our kiss ends with a hush and the sun starts to dip behind the steaming horizon just beyond a row of trees. Autumn's arms aren't around me anymore and she's standing next to me, looking at the last moments of tepid daylight. She points high in the air and looks at me, her glance attempting to tell me every story she knows. I don't know what she sees and her lips move again but I can't hear the words, can't hear what this exquisite woman is saying to me.

Time moves forward as quick as it can while all I hear are only my deep breaths in the winter cold.

Autumn stands in front of me and all the echoes of the bitter terrain are silenced by her eyes. Her eyelids drop and I can finally listen to the supple whisper of her voice.

"Will you?"

#

Carroty streaks of twilight dance into the hospital room and my hand is still entwined with Autumn's. It looks as if she's smiling but it could be the haze of early morning affecting my vision. A nurse walks into the room and marks a sheet on a clipboard after looking at the various monitors above the bed. I stand up and leave the room, the sound of my footsteps drowned in a sea of hurried doctors and medical personnel rushing past.

The ICU visitors' bathroom is just around the corner. I push the door open and an elderly man wearing a long brown coat exits. He has the eyes of a dead soldier. I turn on the faucet to wash my face and only a few moments pass before I see that my lips are blue. I back away and close my eyes for a second, letting the empty noise of the bathroom stalls soothe the slightest tinges of panic in my mind.

A deep breath spins in my chest and I finish washing my face. My reflection is now a warm state and lips have returned to the color of tired flesh. The past two weeks have been a time imperfect and before long Autumn's voice will be replaced by the frightening silence of her death.

#

I take another sip of water and imagine that I'm sitting in the café where I met Autumn five years ago, a dull Saturday morning when the sky was as dark as dirty glass. She was wearing a tight tweed skirt, legs like two pale knives with boots creeping up to the middle of her calves. My heart stopped for a few minutes when I first touched her skin and I imagine she stole my breath during our initial kiss and hid it in the corners of her stomach.

I haven't drank a latte since that day.

The beep of the heart monitor forces me back into the present. I sit on the edge of the cot and see that it's almost nighttime. I haven't talked to my parents or friends in too many days and I believe they've lost faith in Autumn's recovery. The hustle of medics outside the room has waned, only a lone nurse sits behind the ICU desk, reading a newspaper and answering the phone on sporadic rings. I stand up and pull the cot closer to Autumn's bed until the weak metal frame is touching the bed sheets. I lay back and nestle my head against the pillow, taking Autumn's fingers and placing them over mine. I close my eyes and see the colorless void where my dreams melt with black snow.

#

An excess of icy rain at my fingertips and I'm staring into a faultless circle of moonlight. Dead tree limbs hang over my head and Autumn grabs the edge of one, pulls it back and bits of snow fly into the night air. She giggles but the noise is caught somewhere between the stars and my heart. Her hair is like fire caught in a mesh of fuzzy fabric, untamed and flowing behind her ears and neck. She reaches for my hand, black fingernails gracing my pastel skin. Autumn smiles and brings it to her mouth, giving my hand a quick kiss and leaving behind the residue of cherry-flavored Chapstick. I curl an arm around her shoulder and pull her close to me, her wool hat nudged against my chin. She smells like apples and lucidity and my body starts to warm with the glow of the moon.

A heap of blue roses in her lap, Autumn lifts one to the air, its petals shining amidst a blanket of winter dust, and drops it. It falls to the frozen ground and she grins. I stand up and take her hand, warmth against the chill of December, and try to speak. Before the first of my words escapes, Autumn collapses and sinks into the ice below our feet. Splashes of frosty water, and a quick explosion of blue light blinds me. Seconds or minutes pass and she's pounding on a thick layer of ice, her screams muffled by water and air bubbles. I fall to my knees and try to break the crystal sheet but she descends deeper into the water until the tip of the fiery swab of her hair burns out as her body slips to the blackness of beyond.

#

I wake to the sounds of doctors screaming for help. I'm on the floor of Autumn's room, huddled in the corner as two nurses try to lift and shove me out of the room. They succeed and slam the glass slider shut behind me, quick wave of beige curtains replacing the view into the room. I stand in silence for moments before the lone sound of a piano plays a single note in my head. It's not enough to comfort me, not enough to know that the one love of my life could die at any second only ten feet away from me.

A single sheet of glass separates me from Autumn and I look for something large enough to smash it to pieces, but I know they'll only carry me further away if I do so. The ceiling lights gleam like champagne flowers and Autumn's soul could be flying in a semiotic sky.

#

A sea of rain penetrates the windows of the ICU waiting room. It's been three hours since Autumn flatlined and not a single member of the staff has said anything to me. Autumn could be dead and I'm just sitting in a pine chair while figures on a television screen above me jostle fake emotions.

I walk over to the counter and stare at the attending nurse. She frowns and looks away from me, my face a canvas filled with the stillborn echoes of lost hope. I shake my head and point to Autumn's room.

"Autumn," I say.

The nurse nods and walks to the room, motioning for me to

follow. The trip feels like a four-hour journey from ignorance to erosion and I immediately notice that the glass sliding door is open and bare of a human barricade. The familiar sounds of machines whirling and beeping relieves me and even now I can live with an Autumn that will never say another word.

She's even more bandaged than before and I can't count how many more tubes are sticking out of her torso. Bits of red hair clash amongst clean bandages like bloodspots on a newborn baby's skin. I walk to her side slowly, my boots dragging along the tiled floor. The stigma of hope fades into a mess of black and scarlet as I close my eyes and place a hand over her exposed legs, my fingers touching cold, pale skin.

I wish I could see the blue of her eyes. The floor is surprisingly warm as I slide to the ground and glide into another waft of slumber.

#

A miscible sun projects unfiltered light the color of a fresh bruise. I'm a world apart from anything living and stuck between two frozen lakes. My feet are planted in virgin snow and I'm covered with the sticky dregs of a Sunday suicide, fingers and toes frozen between black wool.

The absence of life surrounds me. Wind beeches draped with ice stand amidst a field of untouched snow, a surface glistening with sunlight. I can't move and it's only a few minutes before Autumn brushes my side with her hands, her touch anesthetizing me and sending whispers and shivers of hope through my spine.

She stands before me with her eyes closed, curls of hair falling in front of her face and dangling like liquid flames. Autumn tilts her head to the side and I mimic her. We do this for what seems like months until she raises an unpainted fingernail to my chest. I can move again and I immediately enfold my arms around her tiny frame, not wanting to let go until I can feel her curves pressed against the front of my body. Her gaze is a bulletproof solstice and she pushes me away.

I fall backwards to the snow and ice, my backside to the ground. She lies on top of me and kisses me, her tongue a warm snake in a tunnel of frost.

My fingers jet into a grip on the back of Autumn's hair and I could die like this. She pulls her mouth away from mine and presses her forehead against my nose, waves of vanilla circling my head.

"Will you wait for me?" she says.

My eyes quiver with affection and our hearts beat to the tune of a thousand dead angels.

"Endlessly," I say.

#

I watch the night explode into daybreak and Autumn takes the last of her breaths. Her chest heaves one final time as the sun begins its crawl into the sky. She always wanted to get married at sunrise and this is the closest we'll ever be to spending the rest of our lives together.

The doctors rush in and I comply with the nurses' request to leave. I walk out and sit in the ICU waiting room, where I wait for Autumn's ghost to fly overhead. The fumes of the afterlife are only apparent for a few seconds and I'm quick to inhale them, embrace them as if I was holding onto the living flesh of Autumn.

The head doctor walks up to me and I can't help but smile. He frowns and shakes his head and begins to speak but I hold a hand to the air and nod. His tongue is on the edge of his teeth and I walk away from the ICU and down the stairs into the lobby of the hospital, past the front desk.

I shove myself through a set of sliding doors and drape myself in the light of a new day.

The morning air is crisp and I zip up my jacket, leaving a few inches open at the top. I blow into the air and a cloud of my own breath hangs in front of my face, the glitter of the future twinkling and dissipating within a few quick seconds. Each of my steps hits the pavement without sound, like I'm walking on thin gray clouds.

The coffee shop around the corner from the hospital is nearly empty. The door jangles and startles me, the ringing replacing hollow silence in my head. I walk up to the counter and the barista looks like she's a mannequin, eyes staring straight ahead and arms glued to the side as if she's made of plastic. I order a latte with soy milk and silently wish to fall asleep standing up.

When my drink is ready I take it to the corner booth, drop my blazer on the opposite seat. I peer at the world outside, expecting the morning sun to pop and explode in an array of fiery silver sparkles. It casually drifts behind a row of clouds and a hot blast of air from the latte opens my lungs. I take a small sip, remembering the last time I tasted the same mix of milk and caffeine.

A girl sits a few tables away, her short black hair carousel into a mess like she's just rolled out of bed. I catch a quick glance, the air between us sliced into a tiny million pieces. Her eyes are gunmetal blue and pretty soon her lips curl into a half smile. I can't help but return the grin before taking a gulp of coffee. She looks down to her book and I see gray tights under a black denim skirt, inches of pale skin peeking above her ruby red flats.

I finish my coffee, slide the mug to the edge of the table. The sun breaks through the steel sky, broken slices of light seeping through the window. I hear a whisper float above my ear but when I turn around I'm greeted with the stunning emptiness of the booth behind me. Deep breaths and I stand up, grab my blazer before leaving the coffee shop. I keep my vision locked to the floor as I pass the girl, not wanting to break the stillness between our quiet bodies.

Time floats past me on the sidewalk, distant and wrinkled. I close my eyes and extend my arms, the echoes of Autumn's breaths lost in the morning breeze.

The Anatomy of a Firefly

A blanket of ash swoops across the sky like a dead comet. The burning star tip of my cigarette floats above a puddle before disappearing into a smoldering display of charcoal smoke and razorblade pops. I take a deep breath, take in the Boston evening wind and forget for a second that it's happened again. Clock reads half past nine and a single piano note repeats in the back of my skull.

She was nearly perfect, hourglass eyes and a smile that could frighten a ghost. Firecracker soul and pastel skin. Two shots of espresso, half of a sugar cookie. Her dimples burst with Christmas red whenever she laughed and for the hundred-and-thirty-seven minutes we spent together I figured nothing would stop my heart from glowing with bright purple light.

And then the look. The arch of her neck and twinkle beyond the olive drab of her eyes. Quick touch of forehead against forehead, renegade locks of black-and-blonde hair falling in our faces.

And then the kiss.

She embraced my lips, our tongues dancing near the frosty moonlight pouring in from the bedroom window. I noticed the chilly gasp first, the way her pupils seethed with a black burst of liquid smoke. She pulled back and fell to the floor, breaths colluding together in a machine-gun rhythm. I shouted her name once and knelt next to her, held her slender fingers in mine and hoped my past didn't repeat. She parted her lips and for a second I swore her spirit escaped through the brick and concrete and wood of the ceiling before finding its place in the sky. She sat up and grinned, long trail of cool breath filtering from her lips.

I backed away, all knowing what would happen next. She stood, traced an imaginary circle in the air with her fingers.

"I am yours," she said. *"Forever."*

White fingernail-polish soon dipped into the red behind her eyes, chasm of stringy tissue and pink flesh pulled apart with reckless abandon. Within a matter of seconds the goopy blobs that were once her eyes were in her hands, simmering trail of blue-black blood dripping from her palms and onto the floor.

"For you," she said, and then whatever bits of life were left in her tiny frame dissipated into cold and shocking silence.

#

Georgie knocks three times, pauses, and knocks thrice more so I know it's him at my apartment door. He's wearing black jeans and a tight Metallica t-shirt embattled in a gray blazer. He stares straight ahead upon entering and plops down on my living room sofa. He flips on the television and sighs.

"I was sleeping, you know." Click-click-click on the remote until he settles on an old episode of 'The Twilight Zone.' It's the one where a woman in a condemned apartment is fearful of letting in a wounded police officer for fear he is Death.

I light a cigarette and lean against the wall. "I know, and I'm sorry. But you've helped me before, and, well...as you can see, I need your help again." I point to her body on the floor, wince only when I picture our evening before the kiss.

Georgie tosses the remote on the coffee table and scrapes his boots against the living-room carpet, kneels next to her and shakes his head. "Ten years, now, Mick, and you haven't learned, have you?"

I grind my teeth, let the rage pass. Georgie's here to help me and it's not the time for anger against anyone but myself. "You don't know what it's like, living with this."

He stands up and pats me on the shoulder. "Relax, I'll take care of this. Go grab a drink or something. Take a walk. You need to calm down."

Nodding, I sigh and snatch my wallet and keys on the little

table next to the door. I look back, see Georgie drag her into the hallway. My last vision of her is the black-and-gold flats on her feet, slight inch of pale skin disappearing as I slam shut the door behind me.

#

I'm on my seventh cigarette and third glass of whiskey. A game show is on the television above the bar but the screen is a blurring jumble of dark flashes. I remember a time where it was okay to enjoy moments like these, savor them with the full flavor of life and vigor that come along with being a normal man. A younger couple playfully flirts with each other a few stools down, the woman with a radiant blossom of love on her face, the man stoic save for a smile and satisfied eyes.

I haven't felt like they do in nearly a decade. It's not that I don't feel the swash of warm in my heart...it's that it can't be contained for very long. It's akin to trapping a firefly in a bottle; its shine is gorgeous and balmy but it doesn't last long before death finds its way in. All it takes is a kiss, a splatter of affection through my lips. Seconds, minutes, it's all a goddamn shadow to me. The result is always the same. Shock, fear, bloodshed and death.

And to think, this would all be different if I hadn't died ten years ago.

#

I pay my tab and throw on my jacket, cold nighttime wind whipping at my back. It's November and at any second it could snow. Slight buzz ringing in my head but my steps are solid and focused. A decade with this curse, this unfortunate attribute that has kept me away from life.

I was two years fresh out of college, spinning towards a live-life-on-the-edge lifestyle, unaware that my choices could very well shape my future for the worst. It took an overdose, a mix of heroin and fentanyl, a cocktail which broke my heart and shut down my lungs. I was technically deceased for ten minutes and I can't remember what I saw except for a glowing black oval and two eyes the color of a dying sun. Everything was different from that point and only a week later my first after-death kiss pushed a lovely young lady to shove a knife in her throat after telling me I'd be hers forever.

Forever is just a word, letters that too often mean too much.

#

Georgie's voice is fuzzy, as if he's speaking through a cloud. "Done" is the only word I can understand on the other line of the phone. I know it's only a matter of a few minutes before my mess is cleaned up and the apartment reverts back to its lonely self. I stop into the December Diner on the corner of Tremont and Milk Street for a coffee before finally settling in for the evening. It's a little after midnight and slumber calls.

I order a medium coffee, black with two sugars. The man behind the counter takes my two crumpled dollar bills and while I'm waiting for my coffee a lady of no more than twenty-five bumps into me.

"I'm sorry," she says, red lips and eyes as brown as rotting wood. She tilts her head and winks with her left eye. "I think I've met you before. Do you live in the building on Cambridge Street near Center Plaza?"

I wonder how she knows me, but I nod anyways. She throws out a hand and I return with a limp fish grip. I study her movements for a full few seconds.

"My name is Veronica. My friend Carly lives in your building. I believe we spoke for a good two minutes a few weeks ago. Remember, the girl that was reading *The New Yorker* in the lobby?"

Brain scans and computes my past memories, those startled and broken and real. I realize I've met her before. "Ahh, yes. I do. I'm Mick."

"Well, Mick, it's nice to see you again. What are you up to so late?"

I think of a lie faster than my tongue speaks. "Just had dinner with a few friends. Needed a caffeine bolt on my way home."

She smiles, two rows of perfect white teeth. Freckles adorn her face like tiny baby ants. A black tank-top peeks from under a white blouse. I suddenly forget my body's exhaustion and agree to sit a booth with her. She tells me about her thesis on Paul Auster for her graduate degree, her love of cats, and how she once auditioned for "Survivor." My skin burns with a comforting itch, the disquieting allure of attraction and caffeine swimming through my veins.

#

I pop open a bottle of beer for Veronica and she thanks me before sitting on the sofa. There's not a single trace of Georgie or his work anywhere in the apartment. I can still smell the haunting leftovers of my earlier beau, and hope that my emotions won't lead to the same result with the dazzling woman sitting just half an inch away.

"I really like your place," she says, taking a long sip of beer and placing the bottle on the edge of the coffee table.

"Thanks." As soon as I turn around she's already in my face, bright red hair a spinning supernova prior to her lips finding mine. We kiss for what feels like a year before I realize that my last adventure in love resulted in an undesirable mishap. I push her off me and I'm greeted with a severe frown.

"Okay…what's wrong?"

I search for an answer but all that's left in my mind are a

million dead memories and the thought that I'm going to experience another event in a matter of seconds. "Nothing. Nothing at all."

We sit for a bit in silence before Veronica takes another sip of her beer. I stare at the clock and it's been a healthy ten minutes since the kiss...and nothing's happened. My heart flutters with a rocket verve and there's nothing left to lose. I pull Veronica into my chest and remember that this life was all but a cruel dream.

#

It's been far too long since I've seen the naked silhouette of a woman on the opposite side of my bed. Veronica's curves sparkle in the morning light, cornflower-blue mix of koi fish and rose tattoos glistening with delight. I sit up, careful not to wake her. An odd hum radiates from the walls, the reckless reverberation of bliss. I plug in the coffee pot and let the caffeine percolate while I relive the moments from yesterday and last night.

I hear mumbling from the bedroom and it perks my attention. Slow steps to the bedroom, as quiet as a beautiful thief. Gold shadows of tinseled sunlight dress a bare Veronica, who's kneeling at the edge of the bed. She raises a hand to the sky, intentions hidden behind a demure smile.

"*Darling,*" she says. "*It's all for you.*"

Her hands pull her cheeks from the inside of her mouth and the sound of the very first tear of flesh is drowned out by the anathema of an apocalyptic scream exploding in my lungs.

Shiver

Her skin is a blanket of insipid pastels and at any moment I'll give into the siren of another black dream. My eyelids open and close, the sticky sweet residue of sex still vaporized between velvet bed sheets. She whispers something that's lost in the small chasm between her breasts, words bound by the silver shock creeping into my spine. I can't move anymore and I want her to convince me that I'm dead.

She lifts a leg over mine and a finger slithers along my arms and chest, red nail clashing with my pale skin. It doesn't tickle but instead boils the blood beneath the muscle fiber until I can feel my heart linger on the edge of a beautiful explosion. Her eyes are gunmetal blue and they flash with a shimmer of purple before popping into a gorgeous mess. I want to scream but I'm not even breathing now, my chest heaving in and out while skin burns and melts.

Her blonde hair falls out in disturbing clumps while colorless goo seeps from her eye sockets and onto the pillowcase, instant stains on Christmas red fabric. I finally lift a hand and see the tendons of my fingers pull back and snap, echoing in a room that has dissipated into a perfect black sky. The stars fall and burst before leaving a comet trail of glittery smoke and her body straddles mine in a matter of seconds.

I want to die and I may already be dead but she pumps and bounces until the viscera of my lower body fuses with her golden pubic hair. She erupts into a quick orgasm and my vision gives out, the sounds of her nails scratching what's left of my bubbling skin a resonance of complete distortion and terror.

Right about now is where I should wake up but I'm caught in a portrait of death. Fade to white.

#

Slices of light peek into the bedroom and I'm naked save for a pair of cornflower-blue boxers and a striking smear of blood on my chest. I can't remember the last time I've seen daylight, can't remember how long ago I passed out or fell asleep.

I sit up with an eager twist and attempt to straighten my stiff back, neck. It feels like I've been resting in a coffin under a bowling alley, soft pounces of black sound radiating through tired ears. Every tiny noise startles me and I wish for only a moment that I could fall back asleep and forget I exist.

A small plastic vial the color of Thanksgiving rests on the floor, two numbers written in black permanent marker adorn the cap: **16**. I stare at it for a few minutes before tossing it against the wall. My face buried in cold hands, I take deep breaths and try to speed up my heart. Shocks of warm pain glide through veins and into my left arm and I panic with thoughts of a heart attack at the age of twenty-eight. I lay back into a mess of blankets and sheets, let my hand touch my chest and work itself down to my crotch and inside my boxers. Fingers find a clear, sticky substance and I bring the gunk to my nose, hanging it a few inches away. It smells like a mix of vanilla and old magazines. I'm afraid to taste it.

Loveless nights lead to loveless mornings and my memory is a blank fucking canvas.

I jump to the other side of the room and try to find the empty vial. It's hidden amongst empty beer bottles, dank light and a single Polaroid of the one woman who stole my heart. She has golden blonde hair and eyes that could light a rainforest. There's nothing else written on the outside of the vial besides the number on the cap but I open it anyway. I hold it to the window and pale sunshine reveals typed words spelled backwards within fine medicinal dust: *revihs*. It takes me a minute too fucking long to whisper it to myself.

Shiver.

Last night comes to me in a stream of grays and browns and

there's one man I need to talk to before I take two cold showers and silently say a prayer to myself in the broken mirror above the bathroom sink.

#

I swallow a spoonful of granola and skim milk and resist the urge to destroy the plate of eggs in front of me. A woman in a tight black skirt and hair the color of autumn leaves smiles at me but I haven't the heart to tell her that most of my girlfriends had either slept with someone once while we were dating or held a gun to my head.

I'm more fearful of women than the dark figures lurking in my bedroom closet.

Another sip of warm apple juice and I look at my watch. Karl is fifteen minutes late and not a part of me is surprised. I remember his speech, his deliverance of a new drug on the streets of Boston. I was never one to shy away from a new experience and I bet I was one of the first to throw a handful of twenties at his chest. One pill and a picture of someone you want to fuck. One pill and the thoughts of any woman in the world. One pill and the memories of a lost love. That's all he said before handing over the vial.

My wife's dead and I'll do anything to touch her again.

The diner door jingles and a swarm of elderly women walk in, each looking like she's lost after an hour of church. I finish my breakfast and twirl a spoon in midnight-colored coffee. Karl's the next to walk in and he slowly makes his way to the booth. His head is shaved and his looks like a reformed skinhead that's given up on gangbanging and taken up golf. He's wearing a tight-knit polo shirt with a small pelican emblem and faded black jeans. His eyes are wide and blue like he's been up all night snorting coke or doing his taxes.

"My friend," he says. "How's it going? Tell me you had a great night."

He reaches out to give me a high five but I wave it away with my mug. I take a long, involved sip of coffee and stare at Karl for at least thirty seconds.

"I did not have a great night, Karl," I say. "It wasn't even close to that."

"Oh, come on man. Lighten up. Tell me that it was a fucking *experience*, brother. Tell me that you've never woken up feeling like a dream was reality."

I push away my coffee and lean back into the booth, the strength of my body squishing into aged leather. I've never been awake this early on a Sunday and I already regret asking Karl to meet me. "I suppose it's my fault for trying it. But that was too much even for me. It wasn't really Rachael."

Karl laughs and his imperfect teeth part. I'm sure he hasn't brushed them in a few days. He shakes his head before the waitress walks over to our table. "Just coffee," he says to her. "Listen, brother. The first trip is never going to be clean. Did you stare at her picture before you took the dose of shiver?"

I nod.

Karl cracks his knuckles as the waitress pours coffee into a chipped brown mug. "Let me tell you something, brother. Try shiver again. You won't regret it. I promise."

He slips me a small plastic vial with a single pill inside, purple with pink stripes. I close it in the palm of my hand and shove it into my jacket pocket. A final sip of coffee and I slide the mug to the side of the table. Karl places a twenty next to my empty bowl. He raises his glass in the air and smiles. "Here's to seeing Rachael again."

#

My wife was robbed outside of our apartment. Two men raped her, beat her and slit her throat. She bled out on the front stairs while passersby ignored the most beautiful woman in the world dying a few inches from her home. Police never found the two fucks and it was a matter of days after Rachael's funeral that I lost the will to look for them. She was taken from me and nothing was going to bring her back.

Shiver is two milligrams of hope. Shiver is a chance to see her again.

#

The view outside of my living-room window encompasses a city that I wish would crumble. When I was a child I'd often look to the sky and hope that in my lifetime a meteor would strike the earth. I'd have dreams of oceans spilling over and destroying buildings.

A draft flows through the apartment and I laugh at my naiveté as a youth. I sit next to the coffee table and fumble through a photo album. Pictures are bound between red cloth binding and rusted metal prongs. These visions are Rachael and I smiling, the two of us living a different life in a different dimension and I swear both of us died last October.

I flip through photos of our wedding and various social events. Birthday bashes and nights at the pubs in downtown Boston. I find one of Rachael wearing a tight white t-shirt that's low cut, pale swoop of breasts peeking from a plunging neckline. Her hair is short, black slices in a sea of gold. There's a bit of red in her eyes from the camera flash. She has a martini in her hand and her smile is wry but suggests she's having a good time. I scoop up the picture and slip it into the front pocket of my jeans.

Sometimes the bedroom is too haunting. I could wake up in the middle of the night and find Rachael's ghost sitting at the edge of the bed, pointing to a blanket of stars in the violet night sky.

I undress and lay at the foot of the bed, clutching a pillow to my chest and rolling the vial of shiver in my hand. My eyes close after staring at a map of stains on the ceiling. I try not to fall asleep but my single adventure for the day was more than enough to wear my body down. Sitting up, I reach into my jeans pocket and pull out Rachael's photo. I lock her eyes into my line of vision and swallow the single dose of shiver.

Soon enough the walls collapse into the foundation of the building and my heart burns with the touch of the dead.

#

Her head is absent of hair and parts of her skull push through the skin, rotting bits of bone dressed with gray excess and crimson spots. She doesn't cast a shadow and my arms are tied to the bed. This woman wears sunglasses that drip with what looks like sweat and semen.

Cool airs brushes my crotch and my vision is blurry, a dream world scarred like a film reel dropped in seawater. She runs a hand along my side and the touch splits my skin but I can't feel the blood seeping from the wound. I force my legs to move but find that they're tied with solid black cables. She giggles and puts her mouth to mine. I see my own reflection in her dark sunglasses before she tears off a chunk of flesh from my lips. I can't scream or move and I'm sure I'll bleed to death on this fucking table.

Panic breaths of air and I'm swallowing my own blood. The woman is naked and her breasts are perfect. She laughs again and clutches my cock in her hands, easing it up and down in a gentle motion. She removes her sunglasses and I glance at two empty holes housing nothing but spots of red light. I'm in her mouth now, waves of pleasure entwined with spikes of lightning. She moves faster until her teeth are locked onto the tip of my penis. She bites down and my heart explodes inside my chest, ribcage bursting through muscle. Blood sprays across the room and onto her face like a broken geyser and it's only when the darkness hits that a coverlet of poppies falls from the sky.

#

Ginger streaks of light cover my bed and it takes me a minute or two to open my eyes. My bare body is wrapped in a single blanket and all of the pillows are on the floor, square pieces of navy blue comfort amidst vomit-colored carpet. I push myself out of the mess and onto my back. My skin is sticky and I'm quickly relieved that it's only sweat and nothing else. Before I try to sit up my toes slide across coolness at the foot of the bed.

I slide myself completely out of the blanket and look at my feet. Stripes of blood circle the base of my toes. I pull the blanket away and see a perfect circle of Indian red. One finger touches the center and I bring it back to my chest. It's colder than anything I've felt before. Legs give out and I fall to the floor. I bury my face in my fingers and repeat Rachael's name until it's tattooed on the palms of my hands. I've reached out to her twice and both times I've come back with nothing but blood and desperation.

My tired heart beats a little slower as I walk out of the bedroom and into the hallway, past a row of framed pictures of my dead wife and her lost husband. The kitchen is warmer than usual. I grab the bottle of whiskey from the cabinet next to the refrigerator and remove the cap. I don't need a glass and in fact I don't need much of anything right now. Shiver has only destroyed Rachael's ghost and before long I'll give up on the one thing that could have brought me closer to her.

#

The doorbell rings four or five times in a row and I realize that I'm naked and sitting at the kitchen table, my head resting on its sturdy pine frame. The left side of my face feels as warm as a ten-minute-old cup of tea. I run into the bedroom and pull a pair of pajama pants over my legs and find an aged black t-shirt with spots of brown adorning the chest.

Karl is at the door and he's leaning against the railing of the porch. He has a roll of magazines in his hand, a bunch of white envelopes sticking out of the center like an array of bleached roses. "You ever check your mail, brother? You need to get out of the house more often."

I'm silent and I motion for him to follow me into the house. We sit at the kitchen table and he picks up the empty whiskey bottle. It's not until I see him do this that I'm reminded of the marching band holding practice in my head.

"Wow, brother, doing some drinking, aren't we?" he asks.

"Karl, it's not working." I clutch the bottle from his hands and place it in the sink next to an array of unwashed coffee mugs and dirty dinner plates. "She's not the same on…the other side. Or whatever you can call it. I'm waking up with blood in my bed, Karl."

Karl pushes his chair back and starts to sit up. I shove a hand in his chest and force him back into his seat.

"Blood? You've got to be fucking kidding me. It's just a drug. You have an enlightened lucid dream. You can touch those that can't be touched. You can fuck the girls you've always wanted to fuck. All it needs is a vision, brother."

"I know what shiver does, Karl. What I'm saying is that Rachael might be too far out there for me to reach. The dreams aren't dreams at all. They're fucking nightmares."

Karl and I stay silent for what feels like an hour. He finally stands up and pulls a thick brown envelope from his inside jacket pocket. He tosses it onto the table and the noise startles me out of a momentary trance. "There you go," he says. "That's all of the shiver I have left. Probably close to fifty doses in there. Keep trying. You'll find her."

I can't help but grab the envelope and hand it back to Karl. He brushes it away and leaves it on the kitchen counter. He pats me on the back and smiles. "If I told you what that drug was made of, you'd keep trying. She's not far off."

I lean against the sink and watch Karl leave the apartment. He slams the door behind him and an inch of dying daylight crawls in before it's completely closed. I suddenly think that it could be the last of the sun I ever see and I grab the envelope on the counter and shut the bedroom door behind me.

#

I swallow the sixteenth of shiver doses and know that's it only a matter of time before my heart stops and night falls outside of the bedroom window while an arrangement of stars crack and explode. The bed envelops my body and I embrace the clutter of soiled bed sheets and pillows before my vision starts to acquiesce with lucidity.

A gleam of blue light circles around my head and my muscles start to twitch with fear. Beads of gray sweat drip into my mouth and it tastes like spoiled wine. I don't know if I'm breathing anymore and the moon bursts into a fiery flower of vermillion. Trickles of sparkling dust fall from the bedroom ceiling and I can see through the paint and wood to beyond the night sky. Rachael enters the room and sits next to me on the bed. She's as gorgeous as an untouched corpse and a misty jade glow follows the length of her hair.

A black fingernail parts my lips and my heart finally stops beating.

Suicide Angels

Moonlight explodes into a halo of crimson and sparkles. I bite my tongue, feel the white-hot sting of fear careen into my brain with the force of a thousand dying horses. It's hard to tell just how hard I'm breathing, how frightened my nerves really are. My heart doesn't pound very fast, in fact, it doesn't pound at all. It's just a useless fistful of crumpled pink flesh hanging behind the ribcage.

My eye only a millimeter away from the keyhole, I'm entranced by the terror before me. Abel was mixing a drink at the bar in the corner of his apartment, and then the boom hit, like a hundred pounds of dynamite curled into a ball and thrown through a plate-glass window. My ears popped, I fell to the floor, and there she was: couldn't have been more than a hundred and ten pounds of pale flesh and hair the color of burnt cinnamon. She smiled once through the rubble of broken pine door and eggshell plaster, and then picked up Abel *without even touching him*. She lifted a single black-painted fingernail and before I could crawl away, Abel's torso dripped with the charcoal goo that typically runs through our veins in lieu of red plasma. His thin blonde hair was replaced with spinning gray smoke, and it took only a few seconds for me to shove my way into his bedroom and slam and lock the door.

She tosses him to the side and looks around, her eyes like two tiny dark mirrors. Two tattoos that resemble stars adorn her slender shoulders. She's wearing a black tank-top and tight leather pants. When she sees my big baby blue in the center of the keyhole, I panic. She smiles again and I curse the night for bringing me to this apartment at three in the morning. I look around the room for an exit and only one is available.

I'm either tossing myself through the window or this destructive little woman is going to tear my limbs off like she just did to one of the only friends I had. I count to ten, hold my breath at the last digit. Loud clicks and the bedroom splints and pops. Bits of wood fly through the darkness and in a matter of seconds I force myself through the bedroom window, eager night caressing my backside as I plunge to the ground. When my body hits the top of whatever vehicle was parked seven stories from the apartment, vision quickly fades in a mess of black and blue, the colors of a floating bruised peach.

#

Pulsating waves of static, wind scraping my face with delight. I open my eyes and liquid strands of moonlight greet me with a dewy slap. My arm in the air, fragments of broken windshield stuck in the skin like seashells in beach sand. I shake my head and let the panic escape my lungs with one last giant gasp. I look around me and see the chaos: more broken glass and long slivers of dented aluminum and steel. My head thumps with the recurring alarm, flashes of red shining in the corners of my eyes like a police siren. I can see the fire swimming out of Abel's apartment, the lone representation of destruction in an otherwise perfect apartment complex. When the fire department turns the corner, I push my beaten body off the top of the car and into the bushes at the end of the parking lot.

The last thing I need right now is to be questioned by guys much larger than me, especially after a woman half my size brutally murdered a friend I had known for a decade. There's only one place I can go at this point, and it's Cale's tattoo shop.

#

By night, I'm a bouncer at The December Club, a decently-sized bar off of Tremont Street in downtown Boston. The staff there like me because I never take breaks and I have no problem lifting a drunk off his ass with one hand and tossing him out the front door. I guess another reason they like me so much is that I'm never tired, I never call in sick and I have no problem taking a punch to the face from an unruly patron.

Of course, all of these positive attributes are only part of my makeup because I'm a vampire.

The Ink Station is about a mile and a half from Abel's apartment. It's only when I pass a brightly-lit diner that I pause for a moment and take in what just happened. I saw one of my oldest friends picked up into thin air and destroyed by a beautiful woman who burst through the front door with a vicious eruption. I light a cigarette and watch its rosy tip cut through the night. A long drag and a little halo of smoke dissipates into moonlight. I close my eyes and force myself to keep walking. When I reach the outside of the Ink Station, Cale's lone Hummer is the only vehicle in the tiny parking lot in the back of the studio. I knock on the front door twice, wait for the light hops of clanging guitars and gritty drums to pause before Cale opens the door barely an inch.

"What the hell are you doing here so late?" The tips of his jet-black eyebrows touch in intrigue.

I shake my head and push open the door. The familiar scent of new plastic and glycerin washes me immediately. "What a night, what a night."

Cale closes the door and locks it, then scans me up and down. "What the fuck happened? You get jumped or something?"

My head resting gingerly on the back of the studio's comfortable leather sofa, I crack my neck so loud that I imagine the ghosts in the room can hear it. "Abel's dead, Cale."

Cale nods once, and we both remain silent for what feels like hours. "Jesus," he eventually says. "How?"

"I dropped by his apartment and within fifteen minutes, a little chick that looks like she'd come here to get inked exploded through the front door."

"Exploded?"

I grunt. "Yes, Cale, *exploded*. Like, boom." The great thing about Cale is that he's not very good at conversation, but I've learned to deal with it. We've been friends since I moved to the city, only a few months after I caught the virus that made me what I am today.

He turns on the faucet in the corner of the studio and scrubs his hands. "You need any meds?"

I roll up my jacket sleeve and examine the slits where the windshield had broken into my skin. Most of the tiny lines of open flesh have healed. "No, I should be fine."

"You're taking this pretty well."

I frown. "Abel's dead, man. He's gone. They tell you when you catch our disease that you'd live forever. What a crock."

Cale's been like this much longer than I. "We're not human, but we're not invincible. You know that, Charlie." He turns off the faucet and starts to clean up his corner of the studio. "What did this woman look like?"

"About five-foot two, if that. Pale skin, brownish hair. Tattoos on her shoulders."

Cale stops what he's doing and closes his eyes. "Tattoos?"

"Yeah."

"Were they black stars?"

I stand up. "Yes! How did you know that?"

Cale's face looks like that of a tired ghost. He drops a bundle of packaged needles and immediately locks the deadbolt on the studio's front door. He presses one eye against the keyhole and leaves it there for a full minute. He leaves the door and drops the thick velvet curtains down in the two front windows of the shop. Pacing a few steps back and forth, he turns to me and gives me a look I've never seen on his tanned face.

"What? Tell me, Cale…"

"Sit down." He points to the couch.

I take a seat in the corner of the couch and ignore my instinct to frenetically rub my hands together out of anxiety. A cigarette is what I need. I pull one out and offer it to Cale but he waves it away.

"Charlie, we both need to be careful." He leans back into the couch and pushes his sandy locks out of his face with both hands. "That woman, fuck, I can't even believe this is finally happening."

"*What* is happening?" My words are quick and clear.

Cale takes a deep breath. "We're being hunted, that's what's happening."

"Hunted? Why?"

"I know a lot more about our kind than you think, Charlie. I've been hearing rumors about this for the last two years, little rumblings that something like this would start to happen again."

I'm already on my second cigarette and it's only been two minutes.

Cale crosses his legs, then uncrosses them. "They're called suicide angels. And they're a lot older than you and I, my friend."

I tilt my head in confusion. "Angels..."

"They're almost legendary, Charlie. We've only heard rumors of their kind, like they were some type of mythical creature that only existed in the imaginations of a million diseased creatures." He pauses, then motions for a cigarette. I lit one off the tip of my own and hand it to him. "You ever wonder why our population is dwindling overseas, more so than in the States? Why you never see as many cross the Atlantic to come to the States?"

"I thought it was just an issue of sustenance, you know, the way we need a specific type of blood, maybe the risk of being on a flight without a meal..."

"That's only the beginning of it. Have you been anywhere else since Abel's apartment?"

I twist in my seat. "No, just walked straight here."

"Did she see you?"

"Of course she did."

"For how long?"

I slide forward on the couch cushion. "Jesus, Cale, she burst into the goddamn room and in a matter of seconds I was hiding behind the door to Abel's bedroom."

He shakes his head. "Then she's most certainly looking for you now. Neither of us are leaving the shop tonight. You can take the couch. I'll find a blanket somewhere in the back."

"What makes you think we'll be safer in the morning?"

"Suicide angels are averse to daylight," he says. "Or, at least that's what I've heard."

#

I dream of a million black clouds above a purple sky. I'm sitting in a pool of dirty puddle rain, mud and sand stuck to the bottom of my jeans. A comet trails across the sky and penetrates the moon with a single glittery blow. Ice and snow sparkle into a fiery sideshow of dust and bright green explosions. Abel stands next to me, binoculars glued to his eyes like they were a part of his skin. He removes them for a second and drops them to the ground. The black plastic shatters into a million tiny piece, little shards scampering away like an army of imaginary ants. Abel points to the sky and a thick gray ooze slithers out of his eyes.

"They're coming," he says.

#

I wake to the sounds of humming needles and soft whispers, the fuzzy reminders of sleeping somewhere other than home. I jerk upright and quickly realize I'm lying on the couch in Cale's tattoo shop. A woman with hair as black as tar sits across from me reading a newspaper. She's covered in about a gallon of ink, two full sleeves of dragons, koi fish, roses and skulls. She pushes down the paper and smiles at me, nods at the steaming mug in the center of the coffee table.

"Cale poured that for you a couple minutes ago," she says. "Drink up, it'll make you feel better."

I rub the slumber out of my eyes and slowly sniff the contents of the mug. If it's from Cale, it's coffee with milk and whiskey. The first sip is bliss, pure awareness mixed with a quick jolt of sweet amber. I tilt forward, rest the mug back on the coffee table. I've met the girl in front of me at least a dozen times and I can't remember her name. Soon enough, I hear Cale's voice and I know I won't have to involve myself in meaningless conversation.

"How do you feel?" He wipes ink off his light purple latex gloves.

I nod, the caffeine circling through my body. If there are two things that can bring me to life, it's caffeine and blood. "Not bad at all. I think I'm going to head to my place for a while. Not sure if I should work tonight or not."

Cale smiles. "Take this." He hands me a black business card with raised blue lettering. "His name's Davey. An old friend of mine from back in Philly. He called this morning and told me that something similar happened near Citizens Bank Park late last night."

I scan the card, feel the punching touch of his name: Davey Rain.

Cale puts a hand on my shoulder. "He's driving into town right now. He'll be at the club in the afternoon. Make sure you're there."

I shove the card deep into my front jeans pocket. "What did you tell him about me?"

"Only the things that mattered," he says. "He's been around for a long time...a long, *long* time, Charlie. There's news coming out of New York and Philly about this. It's best to stay informed...and safe." His eyes reflect the pale rays of sunlight peeking in from the front shop window.

"News?"

"Suicide angels." He nods, pulls me aside. "Davey told me that at least three others were killed in Atlanta over the weekend. Two more in D.C. And, of course...one in Boston last night."

I sigh for Abel, one of the only true friends I had. "Call me later," I say, pushing the front door open. I pause when the cool winter wind hits my face. I'm being hunted, we're all being hunted. Hundreds of years of living like unknown legends and now the minutes are numbered.

#

I was twenty-six years old when it happened. I can even remember the tune playing in the club. What I don't recall is who infected me. "Psycho Killer" was ringing in the corners of The Roxy, reverberations of twangy guitar and David Byrne's voice fizzing with angsty glee. I stepped outside for a cigarette, mild summer air a pure signal of heaven. The shadow approached within a second and when I felt the bite, the *sting* of new life enter my veins, I dreamt for a full day. It was like a black-and-white celluloid version of my life, the life that would never be again. I woke up in my apartment, limbs numb and lifeless. It took a full hour for the virus to greet me with dead, open arms. The hunger doesn't resemble anything like that for human sustenance. It speaks your name with the voice of a dying child, whispers in the most remote corners of your brain. It consumes you, asks you to do anything for a single goddamn drop.

Here's the thing about being me: it isn't as easy as find, kill and drink. We're not supernatural creatures that lurk in the shadows. Sunlight affects only those who prefer the darkness. The blood in our veins remains, but when it hits the air it reflects a steel gray quality that most people don't even notice in daylight. The only way you'd know I am who I am is if you put an ear to my chest. You'd hear *nothing*, not even a single thump of my heart.

If my heart could beat, it'd be on overdrive. I can remember every inch of her body, the sweet smell of danger and lavender as if it were stuck to my skin like morning dew. Fourteen seconds were all it took to destroy Abel's body like it was fluffy doll. Fourteen seconds were pastel beauty blasting through the door. Fourteen seconds were death and destruction.

I take hurried steps along the pavement, careful not to knock over any kind pedestrians on the busy Boston streets. My apartment is two blocks off of Cambridge Street in a part of town that's often crammed with tourists and children. Some would say it's not the perfect place to live for someone like me, but I have no complaints. Two major train stations are only a few minutes away, and the highway is a stone's throw away from my front door. If I wanted to, if I *needed* to, escape is only a moment away. When I reach the apartment, I scan the alley before the door out of habit. There's nothing there except for the dumpster and a few stray beer bottles.

My apartment is warm, immediate waves of comfort as soon I step foot into the living room. I bolt up the three deadlocks behind me and slam the door. I'm not taking any chances, even in the calm light of day. It's been over twelve hours since my last dose and my body is starting to ask for it. The whispers are almost real, as if a dozen ghosts were blowing kisses from inside the walls. I shake them off for a moment and walk into the bedroom. I push the bed a full foot towards the wall and lift up the crimson rug from the wooden floor. It wasn't an easy device to install, but a hidden dorm-sized refrigerator is the only place to store my stash. I plug in the combination and two floating rivers of cool mist escape from the hinges. I thumb through the clear plastic packages. The top layer of blood is all O-positive. The dozen or so packs below it are what I need: AB-positive.

The first conversation I had after I was infected was with Cale in the back of The December Club, a place I'd soon enough call my second home. One of the few fantastic traits is that you can sniff out other similar souls, and Cale did just that while downing whiskey sours at the club's colorful bar. He was my mentor, my guide to this new world, this new life. One of the first things he told me was that just blood wasn't enough to sustain our life; the only blood that would satisfy the hunger deep within our bodies was that of the same grouping system when we were human. Since my blood was of the AB-positive variety, the only blood I could drink with any effect on my system was AB-positive blood. Although any type of blood could quiet the virus for an hour, one of us couldn't live alone on blood that wasn't within our grouping system. As Cale would say, "It's just like a fucking appetizer."

If there was one thing that made me clamor for my previous life, it would be the fact that only 4% of the general population could provide me with the proper nourishment. This proved extremely difficult for an abnormal soul like me. I couldn't walk into the streets in the middle of the night with a 50/50 shot of fully feeding the virus. The ones that ignored this crucial element of their existence are the ones that are weak. They're the ones that are constantly hungry. This is why I learned to keep a deep stash buried in my safe. This is why I developed the trait of hording blood in my apartment. I could never take the risk of running low.

I toss a packet of the O-positive to the side and sigh. I take a moment to think of Abel, his infectious laugh, his soulful eyes. We would droop our legs over the sides of the Tobin Bridge when the rest of the world was sleeping. We'd share beers and stories, words that calmed the hunger of contact deep below the surface of my skin. Some would say I could live forever and never know what love could be. Abel was my brother, a soul that would pour you a drink and relieve the tension in your bones with just a smile.

I fish out a packet of AB-negative and waste no time. I don't need a cup; I just pinch a hole in the corner of the bag and drink.

When the blood rushes through my body the whispers turn into silence, every pore of my body dripping with the sweat of satisfaction. I sit back against the wall and let the blood soothe my insides, full nourishment the only thing that a vampire craves more than sex. Sunlight drips into the bedroom window and for a moment I'm alive again, in my head my heart is beating and I'm back with my family. I'm normal again.

It's only when that initial jolt passes that reality kicks in once again. The voices in my belly are quiet for now, but like every one of my kind knows, a pint can only keep them at bay for oh so long.

#

The telephone rings and I shove the receiver to my ear with a violent jag. "What?" My voice is crackly, like it's bouncing off the walls of an old and tired radio.

"Charlie, there's a guy here who's looking for you." The other voice is Mickey's, my boss.

"What's he look like?" While it's true that my body is never actually tired, sometimes after a full dose the eyes need to sleep.

Mickey clears his throat. "Older, but you know, he's one of...*us*."

It must be Davey. "Tell him to sit tight. I'll be there in twenty minutes."

Within moments, I'm in the shower and scrubbing off the bits of Abel's blood that I didn't notice before. I sigh once, remember what it's like to have real friends in a world that needed them.

I towel off in the bedroom and grab a pair of broken-in jeans. Black t-shirt, brown leather jacket. And, of course, a nine-millimeter pistol lodged uncomfortably into the back of my jeans.

#

The Boston transit system is a lot like the fourth or fifth layer of hell: every soul trapped down here is vague of smiles and warmth. Every passenger looks as if the world could end at any moment and it's something they'd welcome. The train shifts for a second and I balance myself with a hand gripping the dirty steel bar above the row of seats below. I close my eyes and sniff. Traces of urine and sweat and rage. I look around the car and don't see a fellow lifer like myself. Another sniff. No, I'm the only one on this train.

I get off at State Street and walk for a mile or so before the sun dips below the horizon. The December Club's lights echo from a distance, its attractive glow alluring and dangerous. I don't even remember what day it is, but I can tell it must be a weekend because there's at least three or four dozen mini-skirted girls waiting behind the velvet rope. Slowly letting them in is a hulking brute of a Mexican named Johnni.

"Charlie, you working tonight?" He smiles and points to the entrance, letting a girl who's presumably underage into the club.

I pat him on the shoulder. He's all muscle, much stronger than I. Any shifts that I'm not covering, Johnni's usually here. Who can complain? It's good money and you get the chance to knock around people who have even the slightest attitude.

"Not scheduled, but I came in to visit..." My words trail off at the sight of a woman with the eyes of a tiger, twisted vines of ink adorning her pale frame. The wind sucks the air out of my lungs for a second and all I can feel is that cold metal keyhole pressed against my face, the eager breeze of death ripping limbs and life. The girl giggles and holds a man's arm, probably her boyfriend. I catch my breath again.

"You okay, buddy?" Johnni puts up a hand to the long line and grips my shoulder.

I nod. "Yeah, just thought I saw someone I knew." I force a grin and motion towards the entrance. "I'll catch up with you later. I gotta talk to Mickey for a bit."

Johnni nods and continues scanning driver's licenses. I clutch my chest, feel the panic swimming alongside the smooth edges of my ribcage. It all seems like fantasy to me; another breed on the hunt for vampires, tasked with hunting us down like fucking rats. I push open the doors, neon rays dissipating into a cloud of cigarette smoke. I scan the bar for an older gentleman but only come across an array of twentysomethings and Goth burnouts. When I step into the lounge a familiar voice slices through the thick noise overhead.

"My friend." Mickey's holding onto my arm, that golden smile plastered across his face like he was a used car salesman.

"Mickey," I say, eyes continuing to scan the rest of the club like a focused hawk. "What's going on?"

His smile fades into wrinkles. "My office, now."

"I'm looking for—"

"I know." He cuts me off. "He's in my office."

I follow Mickey into his office, loud rock music from the club downstairs lightened into silence. He slams the door shut behind me and motions for me to sit next to a sharply-dressed man, pinstriped suit and an aura of prestige. His hair is as gray as dirty snow. The man stands up and offers his hand. I shake it with full force and his fingers are strong and firm.

"Davey Rain," he says, perfect white teeth glimmering in the dark light of the office. "You must be Charlie."

"That'd be me," I say, plopping down into the plush leather guest chair in front of Mickey's desk.

Mickey coughs, then shrugs his shoulders. "Gentlemen, we have a problem on our hands."

"That's putting it lightly, cowboy." Davey crosses his legs, peek of black dress socks marked with white dots. Not many of our kind dress like they're running for office.

Before Mickey can interject I raise my hand, gently let it fall to my lap. "He's right, Mick. I know what's going on. Pretty soon our entire race is going to know what's going on."

Davey nods, lips parted in a frown. "Well, I can tell you for sure that Philly knows what's going on. Dallas found out last week. New York is going through it right now, and well, the whole friggin' east coast is ablaze." He clears his throat and pulls a faded black cigarette from a bronze case. He lights its tip and smoke engulfs the room within a few seconds.

"Is this really a threat?" Mickey leans over the front of the desk.

Davey chuckles. "A threat, sir? You can ask your good friend right here if "threat" is the right word for what's going on."

Mickey looks at me, and I look at Davey. Davey nods. "Tell him what happened last night."

I look to the carpeted floor, try to focus on a rogue patchwork of crimson loops and swirls. "Abel was killed last night. Torn apart by a woman that looked like she could be a dancer here. Short, pale, star tattoos on her shoulders. Didn't even have to break a sweat, picked him clean up off the ground and tore him to pieces." I swallow urgency, let it boil in my throat.

Mickey's mouth stays open. He leans back in his chair and takes a deep breath. "Who did this?"

"They're called suicide angels, or at least that's what the folks down south have been calling them."

"Are you kidding me?" Mickey twists in his chair. He's never been the kind to accept the fantastical, save for the fact that he lives off blood and could probably live forever.

"Listen to him, Mick," I say. I turn to Davey. "Continue."

"They're fallen angels. Eternal souls vaulted from the divine. Angry angels with a path to burn."

Mickey groans. "You believe this shit, Charlie? Fallen angels? Can't be real."

Davey smiles, full grin swooping from his cheeks. "You mean to tell me you can accept your lifestyle, you can accept *our* existence...but you're not open to the possibility that there's something out there even more twisted than our kind? Just think, my friend, of the possibilities." At his last word, his eyes are as wide as tea plates. His voice booms with authority. "The virus that swims in our blood, the virus that controls our every thought, our every action, it had to come from someplace."

"What is this? Retribution?" Mickey's standing up, turned to the open window that looks down into the club. Flashing lights penetrate our reflections.

"There are things that we're never meant to know, gentlemen. If creatures like us can exist, why can't angels?" He reaches into his briefcase and pulls out a slick silver laptop. He props it open and pushes a button below the screen. When the monitor bursts alive with light, he holds a hand up. "Are you guys ready for this?"

Both Mickey and I nod in unison.

"Okay then." Davey fiddles with the laptop for a few seconds and a square box is alive in the center of the screen. He pushes the laptop towards the edge of the desk and motions for us to look at it. "This is thirty seconds of surveillance footage from one of my bars in downtown Philly." He pushes a key and the video comes to life.

The first few seconds are black-and-white motions of at least a dozen men standing, drinking, talking, laughing. The bartender leans over the beer tap and pulls back the handle. As he slides the glass to the man next to the cash register, a rogue burst of smoke explodes from the corner of the screen. Bodies are tossed by an unseen force, a poor patron's scalp ripped from his skull like it was latex. The smoke clears nearly twenty seconds into the video and we can see her: the black and blonde hair, tattoos on her shoulders like medals of evil. She grabs the bartender with a single hand and in a matter of seconds two little dribbles of white fly from his face. He falls over the edge of the bar, eyeless and lifeless. The angel turns to the camera and smiles. She's not the same one from last night but it really doesn't matter. The video stops and I finally take a breath.

"It's not safe in the city." Davey stands up and points at me. "We need to go. You, too, Mick."

"We're not going anywhere." Mickey's voice booms with anger.

"We don't have a choice, Mick." I stand up with a jolt.

Davey turns off the laptop and slides it back into his briefcase. "Some of my guys are in a hideout on the border of New Hampshire and Maine. So far, they've only hit the most densely populated areas. We might be safe there, together."

Mickey pushes back his thick black hair. "This is fucking ridiculous, guys. We're just supposed to pack up and leave our lives like this? And for how long?"

Davey shakes his head. "I can't answer that. Do you want to die, or do you want to come with us?"

Mickey opens the closet in the corner of the office. He flicks the light switch, reaches on the top shelf, and tosses down a large gray duffel bag. "I need about twenty minutes."

"That's fine," Davey says, shoving his arms into his blazer. "I bet our boy Charlie would like to stop at his place before our ride, don't you?"

I nod, place a hand on Mickey's shoulders. "Mick, be careful."

"I concur," Davey says, and hands Mickey a business card with an address scrawled on its back. "We'll all be there."

#

The population hit its benchmark sometimes in the '80s. Some inside sources claimed that we were only outnumbered fifteen-to-one by normal humans. Clans erupted all over the country, some clashing with each other even though the constant threat of being outed hung over our heads like a lingering dark cloud. Although it didn't happen overnight, the numbers dwindled into the '90s. Some, like Mickey, claimed that the scarcity of rarer blood types prohibited a regular feeding cycle for most of the infected. Without that fresh burst of life, our bodies shut down. The virus turns on us, causes our organs to eat themselves in lieu of proper nourishment. Our bodies have the same medical qualities as a dead human if we were shot in the head or hit by a car. Others, well, they're not so lucky to leave something so quaint behind.

When I was a pup, I saw first-hand what the hunger can do to us. A rogue lifer stepped into the December Club one summer afternoon with a gun planted at the sky, lips as tight as bridge cables. He pointed the pistol at one of the bartenders and in a matter of seconds I was on his back, pounding his skull with the bloody edges of my knuckles. We didn't know he was like us until the sixth or seventh hour of keeping him locked up in the walk-in refrigerator in the back of the club. He shuddered in the midst of frost and hunger, his skin melting like cookie-colored candle wax. It took a full hour for the virus to sweep through his figure, destroying every last living cell. I watched in awe as all were left were the burnt edges of bone, a skeletal ghost lain in a pool of orange dust

It's almost as if only the strong survived. Only those who were willing to become monsters stepped outside of the boundaries of decency and planted their teeth into the soft flesh of a human. For some, it was just too hard. Even I found myself sitting in dark days during those years. It was only when I learned to stash, learned to make the right connections did I find myself fed, satisfied, and, until now…*safe*.

Cale was well-connected within the East Coast societies. He knew the leaders of local clans. He knew how to get the right quantities of fuel without causing a stir or raising attention. And, most importantly of all, he hooked me up with Mickey, who kept me well-fed and well-paid with a gig at the December Club.

It's very rare now that I sniff out a fellow infected soul in the public realm. We're an endangered species, whittled down to the smallest number in decades. If you're not like me and you live in the rural areas of the country, I can't imagine you'd be anything but fucked. Only the powerful ones survived the worst, and now the few of us left have to deal with something even more violent than starving the virus.

Everything before this week was perfect. I lived day-to-day with the same routine, the same bittersweet emotion of eternal life. I stay off the radar. My driver's license is under a different name. I don't have credit cards or bank accounts. I deal in cash and blood. I don't have many friends. It's a simple life, but it's a life I've been used to for so long. And now that all seems to be crashing down around me. For once, I'm not worried about my next meal. For once, I'm not worried about finding a woman who I can share my terrible secret with.

Because now, all I'm worried about is *death*.

#

Davey switches the radio station with a quick twirl of his perfectly-manicured fingers. Hard rock, jazz, then silence. He can't settle on a station. He finally puts his hand back on the steering wheel and we continue into the night. We reach the Ink Station and Cale's already standing on its doorstep, plum cherry tip of a cigarette dangling from his lips. Davey rolls down the window and smiles. "Two hours and we're not stopping." Cale nods and opens the back door, tosses his duffel bag between mine and Davey's and hops into the truck with a sigh. He looks back at the trail of fog and exhaust, as if the tattoo shop is his home.

I lean against the passenger's side window, cool glass pressing into my cheeks. Before long, I'm dreaming of the life I lived before all of this.

#

Night burns into a smoldering trail of haze and moonlight. I wake to Davey's voice. "We're here, partner."

I'm out the truck and surrounded by the woods, far different from the world two hours ago. Cale tosses my duffel bag at me and I catch it with both arms. He looks around and shakes his head. "Thirty years and it comes down to this," he says. "Thirty goddamn years."

I can't do anything but look away, listen to the speckles of rural nature tickle the innermost portions of my mind. It's beautiful up here and dangerous at the same time. Only a few yards from us are the booming echoes of misplaced laughter and other voices. Drips and drabbles of other clans, souls lost and wandered into a place where we all might die. Davey motions for us to follow him up to a bleak and gray building that's oddly out of place up here in the woods.

"This place was once used to store my group's supply," he says, dragging his bag over a hefty shoulder. "For years I'd make trips up here with my guys and fill up. Local government thought it was a waste management facility. Never would have thought we'd have to use this place for a safe haven."

The voices grow louder as we approach the entrance, some of them familiar, most of them new. Davey holds the door open for us and we're greeted with a dozen different sets of fiery eyes. These are the hunted brethren, the fellow lifers that have come here as a last resort. I find my place at a table in the corner of the lobby where I recognize Betty, a black-haired raven that once tended bar at the December Club. Her face lights up when she sees Cale and I, arms outstretched and gripping my shoulders with the force of a burning memory.

"Charlie," she says, lips as red as Christmas. "Long time."

A single peck on the cheek. "I know, Betty. Too long."

Before we can start a conversation, Davey's standing on the counter of the makeshift bar in the corner. His words cut through the thick stench of ammonia and fear.

"My friends. We are not here because we are afraid. We are

not here because this is a final stand. *We have not come here to die.* For the last hundred years, we've lived as we've wanted and along the way there's been bumps. We've seen our share of misfortune. We've seen our share of hardship. And tonight, my friends, is just another hurdle that we have to approach with caution. We've lived this long and tonight is not the last time we'll see each other, you can mark my words."

He hops down from the corner of the bar and greets a group that has just walked into the building. I look around, see a set of doors and I imagine this place is not equipped as a bunker or even as a home.

Cale grabs my arm. "I'm not in the mood to socialize. I can't believe what we're doing here."

"I know, I know. But this is the only way we're going to be safe, or so says Davey. I've seen what they can do, Cale. I'll never forget those moments. I'll never forget what they did to Abel."

Cale looks away, sighs. Davey approaches from the corner, two beers in one hand. "Drink, my friends. I refuse to realize the fear."

I can't help but smile. Long sip of alcohol and my nerves subside with a groan. Ten or so minutes pass and I feel just as Cale did. I set the bottle on the edge of the table and slide away into the opposite side of the room. I open the door next to the bathroom and find a storage room, dozens of large boxes stacked perfectly along the walls. It's cool and dark and perfect. Cale's right behind me.

"Don't feel like socializing?"

"Not tonight."

"Me too." He plants his backside against a stack of boxes and lets out a deep breath. He unscrews the top of his beer and flips the bottle to his mouth.

I sit cross-legged on the cool tiled floor, stomach mixing alcohol and the whispers of the virus. It's hard not to ignore its siren but there's enough fear careening through my mind to keep it at bay for at least the rest of the night.

Cale finishes his beer and rolls the bottle along the floor. He burps and tilts his head back. "Jesus, Charlie...we really should be at the club, you know? Mickey booming with laughter, tearing through a bottle of scotch with everyone. This just doesn't feel right."

Before I can speak, the familiar rumble of broken glass and bursting explosions echoes from the room outside the door. Cale's eyes widen, black and blue drops that radiate with dread. I stand up and my brain flutters, wonder quickly if I'm dreaming the sounds on the other side of the wall. Before I can turn the knob the door dents and cracks into a million sprinkles of wood and gray paint. One of the group's bodies is bloodied and beaten, tip of his skull scalped around his temple. Mushy squiggles of brain and flesh goop onto the floor and it only takes me three total seconds to grab Cale's arm and jump out of the broken entrance in the storage room door. I push my way through smoke and screams, quick glance of black-and-blonde hair swooshing into the wind. I don't take the time to find Davey or anyone else involved in the slaughter. I can hear Cale's words close behind me. *The truck...the truck...*

In a squeal of seconds I find the open wall that once stood solid before the angel burst her way into the building. Moment of freshness from the cool night air, soon dissipating into a frantic run for Davey's truck. Cale reaches the driver's side and flips open the door. I jump into the passenger's seat and breathe again while he plucks the keys from the visor. Loud roar of the engine and we're off. I take a single second to look behind me, long wispy trail of smoke and fire spinning from the building.

The truck careens along the dirt road, Cale pressing hard on the gas pedal. The speedometer rifles with glee and soon enough I can't hear the disparate voices in my head. He doesn't anticipate the curve at the end of the road and time freezes as we're spun upside down.

Crank of metal and wood, gush of red from the open wound in my forehead.

#

The stars blush and smile, bits of glitter exploding into long streams of hazy purple liquid. I can't feel my arms or legs and I imagine this is where my soul is trapped. The virus robbed me of my soul and forever I'll be a part of somewhere that has no depth, no air.

I look down and see my boots are level with the sea. I'm walking on water, the glistening edges of violent waves crashing against each other in a fit of winter storm. Snow and ash fall from the sky. When I close my eyes I fall backwards into sand. She's standing above me, hair floating in the wind like a cloud of black snakes.

"The angels form the demons," she says.

I can't speak, can only watch a whisper of smoke escape from my lips. She raises a white-painted fingernail and I'm drawn to the ground, an unseen force pulling me below the sand and into darkness. When I finally shout, my voice is beaten and broken. I hear the murmur now, like a million dead souls singing with their final breaths.

The angels form the demons.

#

I wake to the sounds of blood sloshing against my chest. It's wet and painful and I don't know where I am. Blurry vision gives way to an aura of broken light. I wince when Cale's head is thrown onto my lap. I'm lying at the side of the truck, steady downpour of rain dousing the goosebumps trailing across my arms and legs. I claw along the ground, fingernails digging against a mix of dirt and grass and mud. It's only when I bring my hands to the air that I can see the two events unfolding before me: the rain is my best friend's blood and the light is coming from the fire in her eyes. A suicide angel, the same one from the beginning of my downfall. Leather pants as tight as latex paint. Pale skin, two tattoos now drenched in the blood of her kill.

She stands above me, the rest of Cale's body floating in the air. On the horizon, the last breaths of night slip into the distance. The trees beyond the fence shudder in the wind. I kick off Cale's lifeless head from my legs, his face locked in a cold, dead stare. My breaths are erratic and as she nears closer to me, every inch of every hidden memory of my life before all of this flashes in the corners of my eyes, each scene and every bit of dialogue muddled by the sparkling cigarette burns popping into view with every drop of my eyelids.

I can't see the sun, but I know it's in the distance. I know it's there. She kneels next to me, traces a finger alongside my arm. Her touch anesthetizes me for a moment, leaves my blood in a standstill. The angel opens her mouth and I can hear her words. They swing past the curves in my brain, past the memories and past the consciousness of my mind. Lost and back again. Lost.

She straddles her wet frame over mine. I can barely feel the weight of her backside. She leans forward, lips that could kill with a single bloody kiss. The thrust of a million blind souls drives my body to slide against the mud. She pushes me back down without moving. A long trail of icy breath slips from my mouth and into the air, caught between the moon and the sun. The center of my shirt splits and the fabric snaps. Her face curls into a smile and I know that it's only a matter of seconds before it's over. She closes her eyes, eyelids as dark as wet mulberry. My body throbs and each jolt from her hands twists my veins until they pop and collapse. Her hand stuck to my bare chest, she slides it down to my pelvis, leaving a path of gashed skin and boiling blood. The virus is frightened and subdued. Even its powerful grip can't stave off execution at the hands of the angel.

The hair dangles in front of her face like charred icicles, her cheeks as white as virgin snow. The other hand digs into the new chasm between my chest and stomach. She pulls out a handful of my insides, steaming hot blanket of angry blood slithering away from the mess. She shows her teeth and in only three seconds does she stand up again. My hands wobble in the mud before the bone erupts from below the skin. She lifts a finger to the air and my body slides along the grass until the sound gives out to a wall of black noise.

The curves and lines of a miscible disk of light penetrate my final visions. My eyes follow the comet trail of red dust dancing above my face. Night burns into a cavern of lost echoes, breaths swept away in a muddle of melting static.

The Sound of Gray

A sparkling crackle of wind bursts through the open window in a short fuse of firecracker pops and rogue waves of moonlight. I count to four and tip the barrel of my gun to the sky, watch the cherry tip of her hair fall to the sidewalk like a glowing cigarette spinning downward into a concrete ashtray. Deep breaths slither through my lungs with the force of dozen dying angels. I drop the gun on the carpeted floor and sit in the corner of the bedroom, close my eyes and wait for the broken universe in my head to split through the center of my skull.

Her name was Delilah and she's one of three people that are responsible for killing my wife.

I light a match and watch a twisted trail of gasoline and dust flicker into a dancing ray of fire and crimson. The apartment door slams behind me and for only a second can I hear Delilah's final words echo in the empty crevasse of lies and gray ash under my boots. Quick stomps and I hurry down the staircase to the lobby, past the doorman with a wink and a smile. He has the eyes of a wounded soldier. In only a few minutes he'll hear something pop and explode and forget who I am.

Night tosses a tidal wave of cool air into my face, a blanket of burgundy clouds twirling in the sky like comet trails of blood. I fetch a smoke out of my jacket pocket and light its tip with the final match in the box. Nicotine swirls in my lungs and the moment is gone, behind me like a river floating out to sea. I won't take my chances hailing a cab this late at night but I can smell the oncoming storm of rain and thunder. It sticks to the air like burnt sugar.

Time floats past me on the sidewalk in the form of a thousand blurred faces. Slivers of black static glow with the wrinkled echoes of abandon, the loss of hope bruised into every lonely ghost. I finish my cigarette and toss it into a puddle of ash and rainwater, smoldering decay dissipating into the radiant blush of downtown's neon globes. I ignore the floundering voices in the back of my head, try to flush them out with my wife's sweet whispers. She's been dead for ten weeks and I'm worried if I sleep long enough I'll forget what she sounded like.

I find my way to The December Club on the corner of Tremont and Boylston. I nod at the bartender and she waves a tattooed palm to the dirty air. The elevator takes me to the third floor. My room is on the very edge of the right side of the building, past the ice dispenser and cigarette machine. I slide the key into the lock with one hand and draw my gun with the other. I'm greeted with the thrush of silence. Shavings of moonlight peek into the room and slice the wooden floor into a dozen broken pieces. I sit on the edge of the bed and listen to the odd hum of exploding stars and a moon that's slowly drifting away from its mother.

#

Eyes open to the bright edges of a liquid sky. I roll off the bed and swing my legs to the ground. I peer out the window, flounce of purple sky shining down on a bustling world. Two years since the end of the world and I still can't adjust to a sky that's not blue. I pull on a black t-shirt and stare at myself in the mirror for at least a full minute. Gurgle of mouthwash and a splash of water. I slip the gun into the back of my jeans and lock the door behind me. Another day and another broken heart.

#

Lynne was the first to wake when it happened. It started with a geyser of orange glitter and fire on the moon, followed by hundreds of planes falling to the ground. A steady stream of dark green rain beat the earth and we stayed indoors for what felt like weeks. Lynne would sit at the edge of the kitchen table, fingers twirling the golden brown bangs dangling in front of her face. She'd sit and stare for hours. The radio and television were devoid of human voices, replaced by an ethereal resonance of buzzing hums and disparate clicks and whirls.

When the rain cleared, the blue sky was replaced with an endless pastel of purple, clouds floating beyond the horizon like a million rose petals of blush. Society didn't break down but our minds suffered the consequences of the event. Not a single soul could dream, our slumber padded with the same drone that spilled from the skies and the oceans. Some said it was the far reaches of heaven communicating with our race, while others said we were living the depths of hell on earth.

Lynne and I went on with our lives but it was only a matter of time before her only secret was crushed between a bullet and the envy of the very people I now hoped to hunt down.

Delilah was the first. She was Lynne's other half, her sister and best friend. She was the one who placed the frantic call ten weeks ago, told the police the two of them were assaulted in the parking lot behind our apartment building. I could see the lie in her eyes when she told me at the hospital, each speckle of green lost in the dewy escape of fear. Delilah's tears were as cold as morning frost, and as the paramedics wheeled away Lynne, it didn't take much more than the quiver in her voice to tell me that her tale was wrapped in a spool of deception.

I yawn and intake the first of many waves of black noise from the open sky. Downtown squirms with city dwellers and office workers. I finger the edge of a fresh pack of smokes and hail a cab before I waste any more time. The rusted yellow sedan parks halfway onto the sidewalk and I hop in. The inside smells like a Mexican restaurant.

"Where you go?" The driver looks at me with mirrored eyes.

I point to nowhere. "D Street. Max's Place."

The driver nods and fiddles with the radio. It takes him five full minutes before he finds an actual broadcast. Nowadays, the majority of radio stations can't break through the barrier of The Noise. Only the major market stations have the physical power to push their programs through the thick wall of clatter.

We pass the edge of Boston Harbor, its whittled gray surface rippling in the autumn wind. If you look just hard enough, you can still see the shark fin of the last plane to go down a couple years ago. Boston's mayor wanted to leave the wreckage in the water as a memorial. I strain my eyes to catch a view but the taxi is speeding too fast along the road. We reach Max's Place, an out-of-place bar on the corner of D Street and Broadway. Max usually keeps the neon lights on all day and night and their bright essence radiates the entire street. I flip the driver a sawbuck and slam the door behind me. On this side of town, there isn't much action. It's early enough in the day where I can talk to Max without a barrage of drunkards and whores.

I push the velvet doors open and drop my sunglasses into my inside jacket pocket. There's a few scattered souls spread amongst the bar, a bunch of haggard and unemployed men swallowing their sorrows drop-by-drop. Max calls out to me and I lean over the side of the bar. Flop of hair the color of dirty snow hangs in front of his face. He nods to the side and turns around.

"In the back," he says.

I flip up the bar gate and follow him into the back room, past the kitchen and into what he calls an office, which is more-or-less a small room with a poster of Dennis Eckersley below the dead clock above the desk. He sits with a sigh and pushes a stack of papers away from the center of the table.

"Close the door and sit down."

I do what he asks and plop myself into the plushy leather chair across from his desk. I clear my throat and remove the gun from the back of my jeans. "Delilah's gone, Max."

He smiles and throws his sandaled feet on the side of the desk. "I know. Saw the paper this morning. You should do this for a living, you know. I bet there are many, many people who would kill for someone like you."

I shake my head. "Where can I find the third one?"

"Right down to business, I see." He leans over the desk, blue steel eyes beaming with drops of stoicism. He opens the top desk drawer and removes a thick manila envelope.

"You've known me for over a decade, Max. You know I need to finish this. I know where Doc is and I know I need a few days before I find him. Where's the third?" I take a deep breath, remember my dead wife and the way she would kiss the back of my neck when she woke up in the morning.

Max nods, strokes the fuzzy tip of his beard. "Right here, my friend. The address, pictures and whatnot. Everything you need. I imagine you know where Doc can be found, but this other guy wasn't so easy to track down. You did what you had to last night, but please; careful, careful, careful. I like to not think that last night you were just *lucky*."

"Luck has *nothing* to do with this. Lynne's dead, buried and gone because of them. And for what? Because she could do something that no one else could?" Fury beams in my voice and it's too late to realize I'm yelling at the wrong person. I'm yelling at a guy who knew my father, a guy who's actively helping me track down and erase the ones who killed my wife.

"Sit down, please. Just relax for a second. Your wife had a gift in this crazy new world. Look at the people who killed her. She saw what they would become, saw *everything* that would happen. They thought that gift was too powerful and they were afraid of it, my friend. Fear drives a man to do unspeakable things."

"Not a good enough excuse." I snatch the envelope from the table and follow the trail of music from the bar and out into the street. I light a cigarette and inhale at least half of it in a single splurge. I watch an elderly woman hail a cab across the street. Gunmetal-blue hair, eyes of a tired spirit. I bet she hasn't smiled in years. I shake my head and lean against the edge of the brick wall, forget who I am for a second. When my body falls asleep at night, all the brain can see is black. All we can hear is that same goddamn drone radiating from the sky and from the ocean. My wife, she was different. She could close her eyes at night and nothing was different from before. She could dream and no other living piece of flesh could do so. And her dreams weren't just rehashed celluloid from a weary day. She saw what her friends and family would become. She gave her sister a palmful of news, told her that the baby wouldn't make it. She told Doc and Delilah what was in store for their future and the third man in this adventure informed them the only way to alter the timeline was erase the source of the dreams.

My wife opened her soul to Delilah and the others. And they killed her for it.

#

I throw back a shot of rum like it could douse the fire in my heart. An old Bruce Springsteen tune plays on the jukebox, twangy guitars and a pinch of bluegrass. I slide the glass to the edge of the bar and toss a ten next to the napkin holder. The bartender nods and smiles, wrinkles in his forehead shining in the pale light. Night has fallen outside and still the eager traces of purple paint a sky that has no end. I slam a cigarette into my mouth, silently hope that there's enough cash in my pocket for a cab ride back to my hotel.

A halo cloud of smoke and cool breath escapes from lips and disappears into the night. The October breeze is light and welcoming so I avoid the taxis and begin my walk to Doc's auto repair shop on the edge of town. I imagine he'll be upset and angry, because just a few days ago I grabbed his wife's throat and shoved her through a plate glass window and watched her fall nearly a hundred feet to the ground.

#

Doc and I grew up in Southie. Our families were close and we played little league together. Flash forward to twenty years later and there's half a moon in the sky and he's killed my wife. Back Bay Repair is open past eight o'clock and I'm lucky enough to beat feet around the corner at half past seven. I imagine a man needs time to get over his wife's death but Doc was always one to work through the pain. I have no idea when or where Delilah's funeral happened nor do I care; all I want is ten seconds alone with him.

I see Doc's dirty Mustang parked illegally in front of a fire hydrant. Slow steps beyond the dark street light, past the neon allure of the strip club two doors down. This used to be a nice part of town but nowadays no part of Boston can handle an upper class overhaul. An older couple, man in a blue suit and his partner in jeans and a light pastel jacket, exit the front door and pop into a Cadillac a block away. The less people in this place, the better.

I push the door open and the jingle startles my heart. A woman at the front desk with deep black hair and apple-red cheeks smiles.

"Can I help you?" She turns from the computer monitor and faces me.

I peer into the window behind her. Doc's head of brown hair is huddled below an SUV on the lift. "I'm a friend of Doc's. I came by to see how he was doing."

The woman frowns. "He's holding up, dear. Shouldn't be back to work so soon, but...you know how he is."

"Yeah."

"I'll let him know he has a visitor. What's your—"

The door handle rattles and Doc's standing next to the desk, wide eyes and the look of desperation built into his scruffy face. "What are you doing here?" He rubs his oily hands with a crimson handkerchief.

I smile and reach for the gun. "Now you know how it feels." I pull the trigger twice and the nice lady at the desk howls with fear. Doc falls to the ground and what's left of the back of his skull strikes the ground in a goopy mess. I nod at the woman and head for the door. Frantic steps turn into a jog turns into a full run. When I'm at least a half mile away I collapse into an alley and breathe for the first time in God knows how many seconds.

Doc and I hadn't seen each other since Lynne's funeral. He could barely look me in the eye during the ceremony. Lynne had told Doc and Delilah that their three-month-old daughter wouldn't survive the fourth month. When the couple found their baby breathless and blue in her crib a week afterwards, they blamed my wife. And when Lynne informed them of a car accident involving Doc, Delilah and a third person, they put a stop to it.

\#

The stars lead me back to the hotel. When I walked past the Charles River, The Noise was louder than it had ever been before. It pounced on my temples, beat the sides of my brain with sound waves that could have shattered the weakest parts of my skull.

The hotel lobby is empty save for the doorman and a few scattered women. I waste no time in hurrying into an elevator and into my room. It's only a matter of time before I'm caught and this final character needs to be finished tomorrow. I toss my jacket onto the bed and remove the envelope from beneath the mattress. Two sheets of paper and a photograph fall out. The first is a black-and-white copy of Ramon Humbart's driver's license, and the second is a map to his apartment building in the North

End of Boston. I lay back into the plushy comfort of the bed, let my mind relax as best it can. The Noise subsides for a few seconds and I can hear Lynne's voice. It cuts through the static like music battling on the far reaches of an AM station. Soft traces of whispers, the momentary display of rasping words that are the most beautiful sounds I've ever heard. I can almost see the brown hairline above her thin eyebrows, summer eyes with a tinge of blue.

I force myself off the bed and take deep breaths until I'm back into consciousness. My suitcase is in the corner of the room and before long I dive into it, toss clothes and jeans and t-shirts aside until I can find the crumpled stationery below the assortment of socks and underwear. I hold it to the light, glittery drops of blue and black ink glistening with artificial love. My back to the carpet, I read every line as if it were the first time. It's a letter from Lynne written two days before she died. She sealed it into an envelope and hid it her dresser, unbeknownst to me until a week after she was killed. She said she had a dream and it was only a few minutes in length. It details my brief future and every time I read it the words shake me more and more. I fold it up and gently ease it into my front jeans pocket. With any luck, I won't need to read it again after tomorrow.

#

Dawn greets me with a thick flash the color of wet pansy leaves, scattered tube of crinkling light and dust. Eyes open and close to the tune of The Noise awakening from its calm fit of slumber. My shower is quick and it's only a matter of minutes before wet hair scrunches with the dewy frost of mid-autumn. Gun is tucked into the back of my jeans and Humbart's address is planted firmly behind the center of my forehead. It's only a little after six in the morning and I'm not ready for this day to begin. I walk past Park Street station and beyond the Commons, along

Tremont Street until I hit the edge of the North End. The ocean breeze unleashes its cold grip onto the city and hits me when I reach the tip of Boston Harbor. Soft, dark dirt crumples under my boots and I'm walking over the bocce courts and a baseball field.

The skyline pierces the dark violet sky, blood red clouds looking downward as if they were a marching army. A row of wooden benches are empty along the harbor line, a pack of geese flopping about and sailing back into the ocean blue. I ease into the bench, gun gently poking the tip of my spine. I close my eyes and The Noise is calm, drifting shivers of dissolving static seeping from my conscious thoughts and lost somewhere between my heart and my skull. Blood platelets slow to a crawl, millimeters of anger and regret hovering between the rusted blue of quivering veins. The reverberation of a thousand nightmares tugs at the base of my brain and pulls out every sopping memory of Lynne. I can't remember her face, her voice. Vision blurs into a hazy cloud of fog and orange smoke. My lips shudder and crack, thin flame of saliva and blood spilling from its corners like a broken bottle. The Noise penetrates my bones and shakes them until I'm on the concrete ground, fingernails scraping bits of dirt and lost sand. Cherry waves slap and bite the edge of the harbor and within seconds my mind is crashing.

A thermal lullaby coats my thoughts, a million whirling flakes of black snow amongst a field of broken stars.

#

Fade into gray. I sit up and spit out a long trail of sticky viscera, the remnants of lost time. Blink once, twice, feel the sun's warm morning rays soothe the shutter snaps of my joints. Purple sky and viscous clouds above, signals of a brand new day burst from a hazy morning. Crick of the barrel of my gun digging into my back, I pull it out and remember why I'm next to the harbor. Ramon Humbart lives only a few blocks away.

I shake the bits of sand from my jacket and hair and stroll along the sidewalk connected to the ports on either side of the harbor. The Noise cycles on a repeated loop now, same shimmering wave of static burning into every little thought. I inch across the baseball diamond and park until I'm back into the city. Commercial Street snakes into Hanover Street and soon enough I'll reach Humbart's apartment building. I'll calmly buzz his room number and have him invite me upstairs. When I reach his apartment and he opens the door, I'll make him remember my wife and everything she meant to me.

#

Lynne had a dream soon before she was killed. She called Delilah, who at this point was already livid with her visions and premonitions. She told her about the car accident, the smashing of two vehicles in downtown Boston that would result in three deaths. She said his last name was Humbart and he drove a Nissan, lived not too far from Doc and Delilah. It didn't take long for the three of them to connect, and once they did, it was Humbart, a man whose face I've only seen in black-and-white, to recommend that Lynne's demise was the only way to stop the future from playing out as it should.

Delilah asked Lynne to meet her at the apartment for dinner, a chance to put the past couple months of tragedy behind them and start the friendship anew. Somehow I knew that Humbart was the one who put the bullet in my wife's skull and watched her writhe in a gallon of blood and pain. When I got to the hospital, she had ten breaths left in her body. Ten seconds of life dissipating from her eyes like a lightning burst before the final shock of a storm. She gripped my fingers, chipped black nail-polish twinkling in the dreary hospital light. One heave of her chest, fluffed like an aged pillow, and she was gone. Lynne passed with her eyes open and I'll forever imagine if the colorful vision of me screaming will be forever engrained into hollowed mind of her ghost.

The front of Humbart's apartment building is unremarkable, looks nearly vacant. I scan the lineup of apartment numbers and find his: 125. I push the button and an eruption of tones filters from the intercom.

"Yes?"

I clear my throat. "Ramon, I'm a friend of Doc and Delilah's. Something has happened to them and I need to talk to you."

"Oh, Jesus...come right up." The intercom buzzes and I can hear the clicking of the front door unlocking. I pull it open and pause for a moment in the lobby, listen to The Noise hum and drone before I start my journey up the staircase next to the wall of mailboxes. Humbart's apartment is on the third floor. I find his door and rap two times, one for each of the souls I've sent to the afterlife.

Jingling of locks and shoes against carpet. The door slides to an open inch and two eyes as brown as a dead horse greet me. "Who are you? What's happened to them?"

"Calm down for a second. Let me in and we can talk."

The door swings open and Ramon stands before me. The man who shot my wife, the man who took down two lives with a single bullet. He sees the gun in my right hand and before he can fully react I've pumped a bullet in his chest. He falls to the ground in slow motion. One more in his forehead and he stops breathing. I catch a glimpse of his kitchen before I leave and I swear Lynne's ghost walks past the open window. Before I can think too much I'm down the stairs and out into the open street, past the coffee shop on the corner and well into the void of The Noise.

#

I avoid the scramble of faces and sunlight. Morning turns to afternoon and soon enough I'm outside of The December Club, sweat pouring out of every crevasse in my face. I bow before the entrance, take one last moment to inhale the sweet ocean air that has glided downtown. Two minutes and I'm in the elevator, push the button for the third floor. I find my room and slip the key into the lock.

Waft of lavender and vanilla, Lynne's dormant fragrance tripping into my aura one last time. I empty my pockets, slide the gun onto the desk and find my crumpled pack of cigarettes. There's one left and I laugh out loud, chuckle scaring the voices living inside the hotel room walls. I light it up, take a long drag before I dial Max's number on the phone next to the bed.

I hear a grunting "Hello?" and I smile. "Thanks for everything, Max," I say, and gently let the receiver fall back into place. I flip the wire out of the socket and close my eyes. The Noise finds its way back into my head, ample ginger waves buzzing with fuzzy delight. I pull open the curtains and let the afternoon sky bathe me in its peaceful glow, indigo blush of autumn just beyond the window. I grab the gun off the desk and keep it in my left hand. The edge of the bed is comfortable and I sit back for a moment, kick my boots off to the corner of the room. I pull the letter out of my pocket, read it one last time. Lynne knew it would come to this and never wanted me to know. Even her warm glow is beyond the reach of The Noise and I can hear her voice again, supple tinge of sweet whispers bouncing against the soft insides of my skull.

Tip of the gun in my mouth, tastes like rust and cold cinnamon. Velvet lullaby of pale static and the supernova burst of a single gunshot.

Viscomy

I pinch the fleshy part of the skin between the fingers on my right hand and convince myself that I'm not dead. The absence of echoes in my chest, my heart could have stopped beating but the blood sloshes through tired veins. My breaths are panicked, air wavering through my nose and mouth like a broken vacuum. There's a touch of pink in the sky, a small wound in the few clouds above my head.

Traffic hums in the busy street and each passing car makes me flinch. I look down at my wrist to see what time it is but it's bare and absent of a watch. It seems like I've been waiting for Chloe for years, but the dying sun tells me it's probably only been twenty minutes. The door to the sushi dive behind me jingles on each opening and closing and I resist the urge to walk in before Chloe gets here.

Three elderly women walk past me on the sidewalk, each carrying bright orange shopping bags. Their chatter is silent, I see only their lips move. I turn and lean against the comfort of the restaurant's brown and red brick wall, pull a cigarette out of the few left in the pack. I light it with a quick motion and its rosy tip is my personal burning star.

The early evening breeze is cool and undaunted, grazing my backside with gentle force. I steal a glance of an older woman's cleavage as she walks into the restaurant, the hint of a rose tattoo amidst orange-tanned skin. The word "sushi" is illuminated in capital letters in the neon green sign in the upper left-hand side of the front window. Small bright spots dance in front of my eyes like firecrackers.

Cold flesh hits underneath my jacket and above my waist, startling me. I turn around and see Chloe. She smiles and runs her hands along my jacket zipper, white-painted fingernails bumping along each jagged edge of metal. Her hands are tiny, like a schoolgirl's. She's wearing tight faded jeans, a black t-shirt and an olive green jacket.

You haven't been waiting too long, I hope, she says. You know how things are.

I smile and cross my arms.

She rubs the edge of my elbow and it's too hard to stop thinking about her body for more than two or three minutes in a row. She has eyes that could frost the surface of a highway. Chloe nods in the direction of the restaurant and I follow her in. She walks in confident steps, as if already knowing that every guy in the place is going to stare at her upon her entrance. There's a young couple presumably on a date in the front booth, a group of hipsters sitting at three connected tables to the side. A Japanese new-wave tune plays in the background, a girl with a squeaky voice repeating the same line over and over.

Chloe points in the direction of an empty booth and sits down. I sit across from her and close my eyes for a moment, hands at my sides and stuck to the fake red leather below me. The waitress, a short Japanese girl with golden streaks in her black hair, places two menus on the table and smiles, then walks away.

I already know what I want, Chloe says.

You always do, I say.

She taps her fingers on the table and stares at me, as if bored with this restaurant and bored of my company. You don't have to go through with this if you don't want to, she says. I've told you that a hundred times.

And I've given you the same fucking answer a hundred times, I say. I'm ready, and I'm going to help you.

Chloe bites her lip and looks at the couple in the front of the restaurant. She flips a bit of hair out of her face. Fine, she says. I told Hank that we'd be there by ten.

I nod and look at my menu. The waitress walks over and Chloe orders the spicy tuna roll and a beer. I order the same and the little Japanese girl bows and heads to the kitchen to get our drinks. I take a deep breath and gaze at Chloe, her narrow cheekbones and the small bits of blush parallel to her nose. The things I'll do for love are the things I'll always regret.

#

Chloe's car holds the remains of old styrofoam coffee cups and empty cigarette boxes but smells like a mix of blueberry and autumn. She keeps her hands at ten and two on the wheel, eyes focused and staring straight ahead. The road is a mirror of green and purple light, my mind lost somewhere in the haze of the night. The radio is turned off but Chloe hums her own tune, taking small breaths in between verses.

She stops at a red light and looks at me, smiles. I think she can feel my fear, feel the way that my eyes dart back and forth between the street and my hands. Chloe is a beacon of solitude and I don't think that I've ever seen her afraid of anything.

We're almost there, she says.

I stay silent and watch the buildings pass by on my right, somewhat aware that we're entering a seedy part of town. Chloe turns the car into the parking lot to the side of a rundown apartment building with beige balconies on every floor. From the outside, it looks like a welfare crack den from the late '70s. I never question Chloe and tonight will be no different.

We get out of the car and she embraces me in a hug, kisses the t-shirt below my jacket. Her lips send a shockwave of warmth throughout my chest, my arms, and for only now I can feel my heart beating again, each thump loud enough to split my eardrums. We look at each other for a full minute before she lets her arms fall to the side.

Can you get my bag out of the trunk, she says.

She presses a button on her keys and the trunk opens. I push away the piles of clothes and a briefcase to get to the small blue duffel bag in the corner. It looks light but probably weighs ten pounds. Chloe takes my hand and we walk slowly past the other cars in the lot. She pauses at a red Thunderbird with black stripes and says that it's Hank's car. When she says his name she winces, like something popped in her stomach. We keep walking and head up the two flights of concrete stairs, each step echoing in the night.

Chloe stops at the double doors of the entrance and turns to me, holding my hands in hers. Her brunette hair hangs in front of her eyes like dead tree limbs. Her eyes are now serene, the calm before our night begins.

Remember, she says. If there's too much blood, you can always close your eyes.

#

We're on the seventh floor of the apartment building, just outside of room 717. The tangy odor of foreign foods is prevalent in the hallway, which looks like an endless array of chipped brown doors and dirty green carpet. Fluorescent lights on the ceiling trap various dead insects, a dull shine that does nothing for the mood of this building, does nothing for the mood of this evening.

Chloe takes a deep breath before knocking. Three loud raps and Hank shouts something from the other side. He answers the door wearing navy blue khakis, a Led Zeppelin t-shirt and aged cowboy boots. He could be in his early fifties, a swarm of gray and black hair on his head like that of a spider monkey.

You're late, he says. I want this thing out of my fucking apartment, Chloe.

Chloe pushes her way in and I follow behind. Hank frowns when I walk past him, seemingly not expecting my presence in Chloe's work tonight. He smells like a casino and the rest of his apartment has the décor of a middle-aged bachelor, vomit-colored carpet and a single recliner in the living room. The television is small, its antennas rusted. The kitchen is bright and the ceiling fan spins with delight.

Hank points to the refrigerator and makes a drinking motion with his hands. Beer, anyone, he says.

Both Chloe and I shake our heads and she takes a seat at the pine kitchen table. She points to the blue duffel bag and I set it on the table, a quick clanking of metal when it rests. Hank puts his hands on his hips and leans against the wall, looking Chloe up and down, staring at her crossed legs. I feel a quick urge to wrap my hands around his throat and squeeze but I resist.

Chloe fidgets in her chair, feet tapping the yellow linoleum floor. How long has it been here, she says. It's important to know.

Hank coughs and spits something into the sink amidst a mess of dirty dishes and a single silver pot. It got here this morning, he says. Your friend from Venezuela knocked at my fucking door at four in the morning and left it here.

Chloe lets out a small giggle and winks at me, the plush residue of affection dripping from my heart. Her shoulder blades have more definition when she laughs and I picture myself on top of her, rosy red cheeks bursting with a mix of sexual prowess and unfiltered passion. The vision fades when Hank's voice fills the room, a deep growl that I'm sure is a lot tougher than his bite.

Please, let's get to work, Chloe, he says.

Chloe nods and she gets out of her chair in slow motion, a stellar green trail of haze behind her. My eyes blink three times and I know that four nights without sleep has taken a toll on my body. I shove my hands in my pocket and rattle the change, hoping to wake myself with the slight ringing of metal coins. Hank snaps his fingers and points in my direction. He walks over and places a hand on my shoulder, pinches the jacket and tilts his head.

You look like a tired surfer, he says. Maybe you should take a nap or something.

I push his hand away and follow Chloe, who's already in the

spare bedroom. The door is masked in various bumper stickers and rock-band logos. She turns the doorknob and a mass of insipid light surrounds her, illuminating her body in a peculiar glow. She stands silent for a moment then walks into the room. Hank steps in front of me and heads into the room behind Chloe and slams the door. I can hear Chloe shouting at him and telling him that she won't take out the package unless I'm in the room with her. Hank swears and opens the door.

Alright cowboy, you can come in, he says.

Chloe kneels next to a naked man on the floor, coil springs of the mattress protruding from the spots that his body isn't covering. He's skinny and looks like an anorexic version of a washed up Mexican heroin addict, olive skin and jet black hair. Chloe reaches into the duffel bag and pulls out a pair of latex gloves. She traces a finger around his nipples and down to the center of his abdomen, pausing for a moment to look up at me. Our eyes dance for a few seconds and I have to look away. She pokes the man's sides twice before rubbing the area above his left kidney.

This is it, she says.

Hank takes a deep breath. Finally, he says.

Chloe taps the carpet next to her and I sit down. She leans over and whispers into my ear, cold traces of the world we share. She points to the duffel bag and I know exactly what she needs. I reach in and find the slender, black velvet box and a pair of metal prongs. She gives me a light kiss on the cheek when I hand them to her.

Hank reaches over to the bookshelf against the wall and grabs the rubbing alcohol. He hands it to Chloe, who opens it and pours a small amount on the naked man's skin. A tiny trail of the clear liquid slithers down his side and onto the mattress, falling into a crevasse between pieces of the dirty white fabric. Chloe removes the scalpel from the black box and cuts into him, slowly at first. A woman with a sharp object is the most beautiful sight that has ever graced my eyes.

Blood trickles from the wound and Chloe continues to work, crimson smears on her latex gloves. She slides her hand into the naked man and taps my arm with the other. There's one more set of gloves in the bag for me and it's my turn to reach into the blood. I place the metal prongs into the wound and spread apart the skin, flesh curling upwards like rotten linoleum.

Hank turns away and rests his face against the wall. I can't watch, he says.

Chloe smiles and blows me a kiss. Her hand disappears further into the naked man and her face turns red with frustration. Her eyes widen and she pulls out a small plastic bag, a cocoon of dark matter wrapped tightly within. She places it on the body's chest and looks at Hank.

There it is, she says. Nearly thirteen or fourteen ounces of heroin, I think.

She hands me the scalpel but I fumble it and it pierces the tip of my thumb. I bring it to my chest and blood oozes onto my shirt. The pain is constant and sharp, a blanket of black lightning throughout my bones. Chloe stands up and I wave my hand. I'll be fine, I say.

Chloe removes her gloves and throws them on the floor. She leans down and rubs the bottom of my ear and her touch removes the sharp tinges of pain for only a moment. Hank snatches the package from the naked man's chest and points in the direction of the doorway. You can wash up in the bathroom, he says.

The prongs are still in the body's wound and I pry them out of the opening, wrapping them in a small brown towel that was next to the mattress. Chloe and I leave the room and before we get to the bathroom, she mouths three words that I haven't heard since she's been back in town.

The bathroom is unusually large for the size of Hank's apartment. A stack of yellow towels adorn a small cabinet next to the shower. Chloe turns on the water and a steady stream washes her hands. I clean the prongs and hand them to Chloe, who leaves the bathroom. It's usually at these moments that she'll ask for the money and I always feel uncomfortable listening to the exchange. A splash of water on my face feels like heaven.

I walk into the tail end of Chloe and Hank's conversation. His last name was Viscomy, he says to her. He hands her a small black trash bag and I can see that she's forcing a smile. This must be the way that a strict business mind works. Chloe takes my hand and we leave without saying goodbye to Hank. The hallway smells different than before, more like a morgue than a mix of culture.

Chloe speaks first when we leave the building and reach her car. This next part is always the hardest, she says. I'm sorry.

I remain silent and lean into what's left of her sweetness, place a single kiss on her forehead. Don't worry, I say.

She removes the briefcase from the trunk and dumps the contents of the trash bag. I won't ask her the amount but I can tell that there's probably at least ten thousand dollars there. The dirty orange glow from the moon above, we stare at each other for a few seconds before Chloe starts the engine.

It only takes twenty minutes to get to the airport. Even at this time of night, the rumble of taxis and shuttle buses are prevalent at each terminal, the mechanical noise of beeping horns a near symphony in my tired mind. Chloe pulls the car into the short-term parking garage and sighs.

She holds my hand and rubs a finger against the wound. A few days and that'll heal up, she says.

I nod and pull my hand away. She sighs again and opens the door. The parking garage air is heavy and my lungs feel like balloons filled with motor oil. We walk to Terminal C without saying a word to each other. Chloe keeps her messenger bag tight against her chest while I hold the steel briefcase.

The bright lights burn my eyes for a few seconds then quickly adjust. Eager people watch the vast array of television screens next to the opening gate, all waiting for that special person to land. All gazing at flight numbers and letters like light to the flies.

You never pick me up at the airport, Chloe says. I always have to get a taxi and come to you. That should change the next time I'm here.

My blood eases into veins and arteries and I smile. I promise the next time you're here, I'll pick you up, I say.

She rests her head against my chest and I can feel the memories seeping into her brain, every night that ended with the two of us in the middle of the airport, every night that she would tell me that crying wasn't necessary because she knew that she'd eventually see me again. The sound of people rushing to their gate as they pass by, I push Chloe away and take her hand in mine.

She opens her messenger bag and folds the ticket in half. My flight leaves in less than an hour, she says. Maybe I should start to pass through security now.

A deep breath stuck in my throat, I let it out and walk to the end of the security line. An elderly couple in bright clothing lift their bags onto the conveyor belt while a twenty something security agent asks them both to remove their shoes.

Chloe looks up at me, eyes that might burst with water at any moment. I'm sorry it has to be this way, she says. I'm sorry that we keep doing this to each other.

Hair stands on edge and I can't say anything to her, can't find the words that could define the depths of my heart. All I can do is wrap my arms around her, smell the tinges of lilac and cinnamon in her hair.

Soon, I say. And I let her go, refusing to look back. I've never once looked back at this point. I usually keep walking until I'm back in her car, the urge to unleash an apocalyptic scream fading with each step.

I pass by the men's restroom and figure that I should stop in before beginning my ride home. My reflection in the bathroom mirror reminds me that there's blood on my t-shirt. I unzip in front of the urinal and stare ahead. The man standing next to me peers over with a casual gape, eyes pinpointed at the various stains on my shirt. He has the look of someone who wishes the world would end.

Is that your blood, he asks.

The Ghosts of Things to Come

Her gumdrop eyes glisten in the rogue moonlight beyond our bedroom window. My mouth reaches hers and in a matter of seconds her switchblade tongue caresses mine. She pulls back, finds my hands and pushes them around her waist. Another kiss, another minute where the world stops spinning. Dark sky bursts into a haven of pink and green, the illusionary deception of too many milligrams floating through tired veins.

She opens her mouth and words flutter from her teeth like butterflies caught in the grasp of a hurricane. My vision caves into an avalanche of quick blurs and voices. She floats away from me, past the ample purple clouds in the distance and into the twin suns dancing beyond the horizon.

I close my eyes, watch her tiny frame dissipate into a pale convergence of ice and snow. It's only when I wake that I remember she's gone.

It's only when I open my eyes that I realize that she was taken away from me.

#

I sift through the little plastic baggies adorning the corner of the coffee table. I find the one I need, take a quick breath of apartment air, and lay back into the comfort of the couch. A cigarette burns into forgotten smoke somewhere in the kitchen. I stare at Evie's picture, finger the edge of the photo that's frayed and yellowed. Her eyes look up at me as if they're real, as if she's living and breathing in another world beyond the physical. If I stare into the black sky outside, past the broken stars and bloody moon, it's almost as if I can hear her sullen voice between the absence of wind and sound.

I dump the contents of the baggie into a small metal plate in the middle of the coffee table. The mixture's powdery aroma eases the jangles in my muscles. Tip strike of a match and it cooks while I contemplate my life and everything that went wrong. I fill a needle with the white liquid and raise it to the air, feel my pupils widen as I let a miniscule amount drip from the edge.

I blow a kiss to Evie's picture, visualize her plump red lips doing the same, and say three words before plugging the needle into a healthy vein between my bicep and forearm. The first of a dozen imaginary fireflies lands on the coffee table and for a moment I am everything and nothing all at once.

#

Evie's blonde hair ravages the supple wind gracing the soft tips of our noses. Her eyes and mine are connected, hers as green as fresh holly. She leans in for a quick kiss and this elates me, makes me forget about the poison running through my body nearly 20,000 feet below. We're on a shiny black surface, reflections of our bodies spinning and stretched below our feet. Evie's wearing a tight black skirt and a white baby-doll v-neck t-shirt, hint of freckled cleavage peeking from rosy lace. She shakes her head when I reach for her hand.

"No," she says, then smiles.

Fingers brush the wheeling dust of ash and smoke colluding from behind her. The black surface is slippery and although my body, bones and muscles are at ease, I'm afraid I'll fall back to earth. I mouth "Why?" and only hear the tone in my own head before a thunderclap of static pops somewhere in my chest.

"Not yet," Evie says, blonde-and-black locks nearly frozen in mid-air like tentacles.

A jolt of dark light pierces the black surface below and in moments all I can hear are the disparate voices of violent angels.

#

Numbers. I can hear numbers. *Three, four.*

"Again." A single word radiating from all sides of my mind.

Three, four.

Fade to white. Shapes that resemble faces above me, a constant string of electricity burning throughout my skin as if my bones were made of wire and aluminum. A spinning slosh of red and blue lights easing from the corners of my eyes and I hear the voices of two men. My body is as light as a summer morning and the shapes carry me from comforting warmth into a rash breeze of chilly air. My tongue is dry and when I let it free of my mouth I'm greeted with a dollop of snow. It tastes like the city, cold and distant.

Vision lightens and I can see the automatic doors of the hospital. It's when a third face enters the scene that a stinging shock jerks in my spine and I'm left with the sweet euphoria of complete darkness.

#

"Bennie? Can you hear me?"

Salt-and-pepper hair and a voice that's cut with steel. He's my father's age and I half expect him to yell at me.

"Bennie, open your eyes, my friend."

He pushes a straw to my mouth and I suck instinctively until my throat is coated with stale tap water.

"How are you feeling?"

A noise escapes my lungs that's part human and mostly demon. It takes a few seconds before I can elicit real words. "Fine. How are you?"

The man chuckles and scribbles something on a pad of paper. "I'm doing well, thanks. Bennie, I'm Doctor Harrison, and I'm not sure if you realize it yet, but you overdosed on a mixture of high-grade heroin and nearly twenty milliliters of fentanyl. You were lucky enough to pass out and smash the top half of your body on the glass coffee table in your living room." He clears his throat, takes a breath. "The noise itself was enough for a concerned neighbor in your apartment building to call the police."

Heart beats slowly, waits for my words to speed its cycle. "Great."

"Yeah, you were lucky," he says as bright tip of his tiny flashlight invades my eyes. "We need to keep you overnight, run some tests to make sure your system will be okay."

System, like my body is composed of mechanical parts. *System*, pieces of flesh and blood and bone without emotion. "Great."

Dr. Harrison taps the monitor above the bed. "You should be able to go home in just a few days. I'll be by check on you later in the day." And with that, he leaves the room, leaving me alone with a mess of tubes, blankets and my own jagged thoughts. I try to sit up but a filament of red-hot pain stings my back and chest. I imagine I almost died and for what it's worth I held Evie in my arms for just a few seconds.

I'd relive the nightmare in a heartbeat just to see her again.

#

The clock in the corner of the room died at midnight. I find the source of the wires and tubes connected to my body and shake them to see if I'm dreaming. My heart trips a painful beat and I'm shoved into full awareness. A quick tug on the clear tube and it pops from my wrist. The ones on my chest force me to grind my teeth until they're off and on the tiled floor below. I find my clothes in the hospital room closet. Jeans, black t-shirt, and a leather jacket that's almost as old as I am. I find my boots in the corner, tie them up and fish my wallet from my inside jacket pocket. Enough cash for a cab and maybe a pack of smokes.

I peek around the corner, wait for two nurses to skitter into another unit before walking to the ninth-floor lobby. No one sees me before I press the 'down' button, and it's only when I catch my reflection in the steel elevator doors do I see a ruffled set of black angel wings and quick halo glittering and disappearing before the elevator rings with delight.

#

I follow the moonlight from the taxi to the apartment complex's lobby. An elderly woman walks out as I head in and in my mind she says good morning. Quick jog up the stairs, feel the pinch of whatever chaos has rained havoc within my chest with every single step. I fumble for my keys, find them buried amongst some hard candy and some loose change.

My apartment seems foreign, as if someone's replaced all the furniture with that of another residence. I drop the keys somewhere on the carpet, hope that I'll never have to leave these walls ever again without the soft embrace of her hands, the voice that could send a slight shiver throughout every drop of spinal fluid. I toss my jacket next to the mess of broken glass and stale drugs in the center of the living room, forget for a second that I shot up enough juice to topple a demon just earlier today.

The kitchen is damp and inviting. A quick flash of my past, Evie and I sitting and laughing and drinking wine, comes and goes without sound and in black-and-white. It could be a fictional memory that's been implanted in my skull. Close and open my eyes, then silence and the same dark kitchen as before. The freezer holds a square container of ice cubes, a bottle of vodka that could be a couple of years old, and something else wrapped in a brown paper lunchbag.

I snatch the package from the freezer and my muscle fibers are already shaking with anticipation. Cool gel between my fingertips, a divine lollipop that contains more fentanyl than I injected during the event in the living room. It tastes like rust and regret, the subtle hints of a life gone awry. I slide against the fridge until the kitchen walls begin to melt and the foundation of the house begins to collapse to make room for a hundred falling comets.

#

The shadows hold secrets and when I open my arms she feels real. She scoops my hands in hers and looks at me with eyes that dissolve the frosty layer of rock covering my heart. My head is locked into place and when I try to look down Evie tilts my head towards hers, forcing her lips to unite with mine until the sweet taste of amber and hope drips from the corners of my mouth. The black surface is now replaced by an endless blanket of gray grass, high stalks sway ever-so-gently in a calm winter breeze. Flakes of snow as violet as dying orchids drop from above.

"Here," I say, place my hand onto her chest. A soft return of tranquil beats soothingly twitches against what's left of the skin on my hands, the pink of our flesh beginning to fritter away, replaced by a translucent covering that barely hides the glowing bone structure beneath.

"Yes, and now, and forever." Evie smiles and in just a few seconds the grass is gone, the sky now a hearty gold. I let go of her hands and close my eyes, picture the previous vessel slumped against a plaster wall, his eyes open even now. Evie holds my hand as I take one last look the world below us. The face of my body is smiling, even in death.

We walk together past the flurries of winter, past the rolling hills and into the golden sky.

Saffron

I stare at the infinite gray cement and pretend I'm an angel. Sixteen hours in the basement of a man that's been dead longer than I care to remember, the echoes of every ghost floating above me like a symphony in this mad new world. My spit tastes as stale as rust and soon enough my mouth will fill with the smoky taste of a fresh hot bullet. Cold metal in my fist like it's a part of my flesh, I take a few deep breaths and remember what she smelled like, the salty wisps of lavender and a smile that could knock out a cowboy.

Her name was Mandy and she was my wife. We were sleeping when it all first happened and now I imagine her soul is trapped in whichever dream was dancing in her mind at the time, the lush purple sky of an imaginary autumn afternoon. I sigh, bits of dust and blood spinning from my lungs like wet strands of red tissue paper. At any moment the moon will rise, a new day dawning over a dying world.

I stand up, feel the tired muscles in my legs twist and whine. We fled from them as fast as we could, the hordes of the dead pacing just us as we left what was our home for the last ten years. The depths of my nightmares came to life last night and I'm afraid if I look into a mirror the whites of my eyes will be a mix of red and black.

I silently count to fifty and close my eyes, hope that when I open them I'll wake up next to Mandy. Maybe wake up with the bright sun shining, pale October clouds floating through a helpless sky. I open my eyes and the stench is the first thing to wake my mind from a momentary trance. They're getting closer to me. I pick up the gun, hold it to the side of my head. Yesterday morning I couldn't have dreamt of something like this happening, couldn't dream of a day where everyone I knew would be ripped to shreds. I can still hear the screaming, the bloodletting of a million souls trapped in Hell.

Yesterday was my last day on earth. Yesterday was the last time I'd see Mandy's gunmetal-blue eyes twinkle with hope. Yesterday was the day God had an aneurysm. Yesterday God had a fucking heart attack.

Yesterday seems like a thousand years ago.

#

It started with a flash in the sky, like a comet exploding into a million pieces of fiery silver glitter. The clock in our bedroom stopped at 4:14am. The crunching of metal filled the new morning air like a soundtrack from the apocalypse. It was only when I looked out the bedroom window that I saw the first plane fall from the sky like a bird hunted on a crisp fall day. It slammed into a house just around the block from ours, giant metal tube flattening the foundation like it was made of styrofoam. I gasped, felt the air draw from my lungs with one quick swoop. Blood rushed to my brain at the speed of a thousand blind horses. I stumbled backward until I could feel the soft linens of our bed, Mandy's toes curled underneath.

"Honey? What is it?" Mandy's voice hinted at the lingering depths of slumber still hidden in her eyes.

I couldn't say a word, could only point out the bedroom window. Mandy slipped out of bed, oversized black t-shirt ending in the middle of her milky pale thighs. I could see it in her face, the dozens of explosions reflecting in the endless blue of her eyes. She drew a hand to her mouth, and then looked at me with the look of desperation. I grabbed her hand and mouthed the word "basement," each of us running down both sets of stairs and slamming the door behind us. Deep breaths forced from our lungs, I shook my head and stared at the basement floor, hoping to find some sort of answer in the dank and dusty concrete just below our feet.

Mandy behind me, I peered out the tiny basement window. Carnage filled the streets and it took me a full minute to realize that the haggard figures in the road were attacking my frightened neighbors. I watched as Doris, the kind elderly woman who often invited us over for coffee, pleaded with a rotting creature as it planted its hands on her shoulders. What happened next pulled tears from both Mandy's and my eyes: the figure dug its hands into Doris' face with absolute eyes, fingers hidden deep within her cheekbones as our neighbor shrieked with her final breaths of life. I had to look away as it brought the dripping flesh to its mouth and clamped its teeth together. Just as it leaned down to feed more, I could see another plane land from the sky and strike the ground with a cosmic burst of fire.

"Kal, Jesus, Kal..." Mandy couldn't form a single full sentence and at this point I didn't expect her to.

"Calm down for a second, baby, please." I needed a few seconds to think. Just a few seconds to process the sights we both had just experienced. "Let's just calm down..."

Part of me believed we were both dreaming. Part of me thought that we both died in our sleep and this was our purgatory. But a part of me knew we were doomed. I held Mandy in my arms for what felt like hours, maybe days. Before long I forced us from the ground and urged her to find warmer clothes in the dryer. What scared me the most was the way she was quiet, the way she would look away me from me as if I were already dead.

I sifted through the laundry basket and found a pair of jeans and a black hooded sweatshirt. Mandy dressed herself in jeans and a bright red thermal shirt. I let the arms of the sweatshirt slide to my palms. Bringing them to my face, the smell of cheap detergent and flowers almost drew me away from the scene. It was only a matter of seconds before I could smell *them*.

The first of the horde banged on the basement door repeatedly, each sullen knock causing Mandy to twitch with fear.

"Kal, what the hell is that?!"

"Stay there," I said, brain ringing with lost memories and thoughts of any basement items that could be used as weapons. The next loud noise nearly tripped me, untied sneaker laces caught beneath my struggling feet. I grabbed a heavy shovel from the corner of the basement only a few seconds before the first one forced down the basement door, its scraggly legs falling down the stairs in rapid fashion.

"KAL!" Mandy's eager shouts sent shivers between my lips. The first of the figures nearly grabbed hold of her before I let the shovel loose in a quick swing, its metal tip catching its decaying face. The only thing I noticed was that it didn't bleed; the only liquid to fall from its new wound was black and oily. Mandy slid herself away from the corpse and grabbed hold of my sweatshirt, white-painted fingernails digging deep into the soft confines of my sides. More of them had fallen into the basement, each tumble strong enough to disable any normal human but not these rotting figures.

The odor of the undead was overpowering, each new body in the room forcing the bile from my insides to slither into my throat. I swallowed hard, stale taste of fear and defeat beginning to drip from the back of my tongue.

I counted four moving bodies in the room. The fifth one stood at the top of the basement staircase, as if in a departed trance. I expected the next explosion to be another plane fallen from the sky, but the spraying of bits of skull and gray matter told me that a bullet had found the head of the nearest figure to us.

"Move!" The voice boomed in the dead basement air. The next gunshots shattered the tension in only a few seconds, two of the three remaining figures falling to the ground in one undying lump. Mandy and I looked to the top of the staircase to see a man with short gray hair and the eyes of a hunter. He trotted down the stairs with reckless abandon, and before he reached the bottom of the staircase the stench closest to us turned to him. I buried the end of the shovel into the back of its skull, felt the hardened and rusted edges squishing into a heap of wormy brains. The corpse moaned an unearthly groan, whatever dying soul inhabiting its putrid form escaping with one final gasp. The body fell to the ground amidst its silent brethren, the foggy waves of gunpowder and rage sifting through the now quiet basement.

The man extended a meaty paw and smiled, two rows of perfect white teeth gleaming back at us. "Name's Jimmy," he said as I took his hand. "What do you think of all this?" He pointed in a circular motion and I couldn't tell if he was talking about the corpses that just attacked us or the fact that the world seemed to be falling apart.

"Thanks," was I all could muster. Mandy hid behind me like a schoolgirl afraid of thunder, chin barely touching the tip of my sweating shoulder. "What's going on out there?"

Jimmy chuckled. "You haven't been awake very long, have you?"

I curled my lips into an angry pout. "No."

He shook his head and wiped his face with the back of his hand. He walked over to the basement window, slid a finger against the dusty pane. "The world's gone mad...that's what's happened."

I nodded once, heart beating more slowly than before the horde attacked us. I gripped Mandy's hand with mine and kissed her on the forehead. "You should sit down for a while."

"No." Jimmy turned to us, smile now faded from his face like he was a completely different man. "We can't stay here. You guys are lucky it was this house I stopped at for supplies. You'd both be—a..."

"Dead." I clenched my teeth so hard I could taste the blood rushing to my gums. "I get it."

"Where are we going to go?" Mandy asked, leaning against the basement wall. It was hard not to see the beauty and hope in her face, long strands of blonde hair falling over her forehead like golden ice.

Jimmy pointed the gun in the air, one eye closed. "I live about twenty minutes from here. My basement is a lot sturdier than this. And I probably have enough food and water down there to last us a couple weeks." The smile returned to his face.

"Can I pack anything?" Mandy inched forward, eyelashes hiding only the hints of terror in her mind. "There's so much stuff I should bring..."

Jimmy nodded. "I'll lead you guys upstairs. Be careful and stay behind me. Those fucking things are everywhere." He placed his boot on the edge of the first stair. "And it's not going to be easy as it was here to get rid of them."

#

Jimmy stood at the edge of the bedroom doorway, back to us and fingers gripping his gun. I had only known him for about fifteen minutes and already he made me feel safe. Mandy and I quickly packed a single duffel bag with some t-shirts, jeans and toiletries. She picked up her watch from the dresser and the look on her face told me that if she could, she would have packed the entire house as to not leave any memories lingering behind.

"Let's get moving, guys," Jimmy said, ice cold stare planted on his face.

We followed him down the stairs and through the kitchen. He flipped his car keys out of his leather jacket and threw them at me. I caught them in mid-air and tilted my head. "Someone's gotta drive...and someone's gotta shoot," he said.

We ran out of the house, red streaks on his black Camaro a sweet sign of immediate comfort. The only thing I noticed before hopping into the front seat of the car was the new odor gripping my nostrils. It wasn't the smell of death, like it was in our basement. Syrupy dew stuck to the fog, a scent reminiscent of saffron. I took a moment to inhale before Jimmy screamed at me to get into the car.

Mandy slammed the backseat door at the same moment I fired up the ignition. The engine purred with delight, the sounds of a dying world buried beneath the moaning vehicle. We could see the lingering figures stumbling about the neighborhood, some running after the remaining living and others dragging their lifeless limbs behind them in some sort of death march. In the rearview mirror, Mandy's eyes were glued to the sky above.

"The clouds," she said, "they're so beautiful."

Jimmy stuck his head out of the open passenger side window and slowly brought it back in. "They're...purple," he whispered to himself.

I stopped the car in the middle of the road, the only walking corpse now hundreds of yards behind us. I shifted the car into park and looked out the window and up at the sky. Mandy was right; the clouds were beautiful. Fair streaks of black and green dressed each steel-colored cloud, bright blue of the morning sky replaced with an endless wash of green. It were almost as if a painter dipped the earth into a bucket of mixed paint and shook the globe until the colors ran and dripped down the sides.

"Kal, please get back in the car. We're wasting time." Jimmy did not look at me as he said the words, only stared straight ahead.

I took a final look at the sky and remembered that if anything, this was a nightmare in which I might never awake.

#

The day's events never fully entered my mind until five minutes into our drive. The flesh-eating figure across the street, the explosions, the attack, even the goddamn sky...none of it had pierced the sticky viscera around my tired brain. It was only when we passed the wreckage of a plane did it all fully sink in. I slowed the car to only ten miles per hour, eyes glued to the mangled metal laid out in front of us. Limbs were scattered about, portions of plaid seat cushions and jumbled planks of steel resting as if they had been there for a lifetime.

The odd hum of the stars above us, I pushed down on the gas pedal just as fast as my heart could start beating again.

#

We pulled in front of Jimmy's house and quickly followed him inside. I was surprised that there were no signs of struggle at this place, no signs of the rotting figures trying to break in. He slid the key into the door in a matter of seconds, the alluring smell of *home* the first thing that greeted us. Jimmy locked the door behind us, eye glued to the peephole. He sighed and closed his eyes. "I'm not taking my chances on the first floor," he said. "The basement entrance is down the hall. You and Mandy head down there and wait for me. I need to grab a few things before we settle in."

I nodded and gripped Mandy's hand. We jogged to the basement door, pulled it open and flung the duffel bag. It struck the ground before I could flip on the light switch. Mandy hurried down the stairs and I followed her, breaths absent of grace and chest as tight as the ringing in my ears.

We sat on the dusty leather sofa below the lone basement window. Mandy rested her head on my shoulder and before long I could hear her breaths crawl to the pace of slumber. Even Jimmy's slamming of the basement door couldn't wake her. I stared at her cheeks, which were Christmas red. I imagined that she was dreaming about better days.

I left her on the couch and followed Jimmy to the corner of the basement. He handed me a gun and took a deep breath. "It's about survival now. For the past few hours I've barely thought clearly, like maybe I was hallucinating all of this."

I knew the feeling. "What are we going to do?"

Jimmy shook his head, peppered stubble curled into a frown. "I don't know. I just don't know."

"How did all of this start?"

Jimmy sat on a barstool that could have been made before I was born. "I heard a few minutes of someone on the radio before all communication went dead. They saw the same things we saw: planes dropping like flies, explosions in the sky…and the rising dead."

"Jesus." I took a deep breath, tried to picture my life before this.

"This is it for us, humans," Jimmy said. "These are the final days. The end of times."

All I could do was nod, hints of weariness pinching at the back of my mind. I joined Mandy on the couch and in only a few minutes, I was dreaming of the same things as she.

#

I twinkled my nose, remembered the smell. A loud crash, then Jimmy screaming. Gunshots fired and one of the light bulbs burst. The night bled dark into terror, and soon enough the stench was familiar. I jumped off the couch and grabbed Mandy, who shouted at the sight of at least four figures. I couldn't believe that not one of us had heard them bust into the house, even bust down the basement door. They crept onto us like the shadows of the dead, the lost souls that reinvigorated every rotting corpse in every swollen graveyard.

The closest one to Jimmy easily overpowered him, grabbing his throat with one hand and piercing the aging flesh of his forehead with its sharp teeth. The bulbous mass that was Jimmy's eyeball pulsated with a final twitch before ounces of crimson goop spilled from the socket. Another pounced on his falling body, mess of black greasy hair hiding the feeding. It raised its head, skeletal face wriggling with strands of fresh pink flesh.

I fired a shot at one of them, the bullet catching the figure in the head and sending it to the ground. Its fellow corpse immediately ran after me, bits of Jimmy's face wriggling in its gaping mouth. Another gunshot and it slowed, stray bullet connecting with the figure's shoulder. Mandy shouted from behind me and I turned to protect her, tried to drag her into the corner with me. Two more shots fired and one more went down, with the other two leering just a few inches from us, eager gray faces pure representations of Hell.

I didn't expect to feel the first bite, or even feel the horrible sting of its claws upon my forearm. The gun fell from my hands and as I drooped over to shove the corpse away, Mandy's scream reverberated in my bones, the faint traces of hope dissipating from her lungs like a million dead flies flapping away into the night. I turned to see her fall to the ground, flailing arms trying to swat away the figure's angry attack. She was helpless from its aggression, crooked yellow teeth sinking into her flesh as if her skin were as soft as vanilla cake. My heart sunk in my chest and just as I freed myself from the corpse's grasp, the shape lurched itself upon her again, tearing away the lining of flesh along her neck. I reached for the gun, felt its cool metal handle in my hands as I fired off a single shot into the figure's head, explosion of bone and brain splattering against the concrete wall. I kicked my attacker in the chest, sending it to the ground with a lengthy groan. One bullet was all I needed to end its hungry assail.

I dropped to Mandy's side, watched the most striking woman in the world bleed out in my arms. Long, chunky bits of blood adorned her hair. Her breaths slowed to a crawl and before I could utter the three words she needed to hear, the life drifted from her eyes like a ghost floating to the sky.

#

I sit here with the gun in my hand and wonder if any more of them will creep down the staircase, the fervent hunger glowing in their jet black eyes. Blood sloshes through my veins with a slight chug and at any second my heart might give out. After Mandy passed, I turned on the radio hidden atop one of the many shelves in the basement. The crackling voice faded in and out, infinite array of static and black noise a deranged sonata in my weary mind.

The voice said something about the sun, something about an endless winter. It spoke of death and destruction, the demise of mankind. The voice soon dropped out and I was left with only my own thoughts and a thousand bittersweet memories.

I walk over what's left of Jimmy's body, hope that some living character somewhere will say a silent prayer for him and my dead wife. Resting my arms on the windowpane, I stare into the black of day and wonder if the sun is really gone. Even if I don't pull the trigger on myself, even if those things don't tear my flesh from the bone...there's nothing worth living for.

I take a deep breath and slide down the concrete wall until I'm sitting on the ground. The gun to my head, I think of Mandy. I think of yesterday morning and the hours curled up in bed, warmth of her soul swimming through the bedsheets. Finger kisses the trigger and the gun doesn't feel so heavy anymore.

I only hope that when the metal pierces my skull I'll wake from the nightmare with her sleeping next to me, the gentle breeze of another day floating above our bodies like the spirits of the dead.

Wither

When I was a child, I'd often close my eyes and feel solace and safety in the darkness of my mind. There were times when I could sit on the plushy sofa next to the living room's window, my eyes closed tightly, blocking out the world around me. The wind attacking the window pane, whipping at the glass, bits of sand and dirt trying to break through.

I must have been close to eleven years old the last time I had done this. My father's funeral finally over, I sat on the purple sofa, fingering the golden trim around the arm. I couldn't hear my relatives talking about how good of a man he was, how much of a provider he had been for his family. All I heard were those tiny bits of sand and dirt being tossed at the window.

Twenty years later, I'm sitting here again. The sofa envelops my body and I'm at ease. Aunt Judi on her deathbed two floors above, the feeling of loss had already gripped the entire house. Put an ear to the chipped paint of the hallway walls, and you could hear the whispers of the dead. My mother used to always say that having a nun in the family was like having God that much closer to us all. "His gentle touch comes through your aunt, Castor. Listen to her," she would always tell me as a child.

I never agreed, as Judi never embodied anything 'gentle' in the slightest sense. My fondest memories of her include a bony finger pressed into my chest, her raspy words being preached into my face. Now, the cancer eating away at her body, she laid two floors above, ready for whatever her maker has planned for her.

Night had fallen and my mother was making dinner in the kitchen. Her brother had just arrived, my cousins unpacking their luggage in the two guest rooms upstairs. No one was comfortable enough to take the second flight of stairs to Judi's room. My mother was the only one brave enough to visit, along with the nurse, who would come by three times a day. Outside, the spring rain attacked, coming down hours at a time. Gregory and J.C. sat on the couch across from me in silence, casually taking deep breaths and looking outside at the downpour.

My uncle Harold paced back and forth in front of the fireplace. My mother sat at the kitchen table with a cup of coffee in front of her, today's newspaper unread. I had been back home for two days, and I was still the only one to sit on the purple sofa next to the window.

"Castor, can you make sure that Judi's window is closed in her room?" My mother was beginning to flip through the newspaper.

"Sure."

When Judi was first taken to the house from St. Mary's Church last week, the convent requested to put her in the guest room on the third floor, which only had a small bathroom and a single window.

They didn't give us a reason why.

My mother had joked, "She'll want to spend her final days as close to Heaven as possible." There was nothing heavenly about the woman.

I opened the door to her room and immediately felt a rush of awkwardness grip my body. A large silver cross hung just above the headboard of the bed, the lone decoration in the most bare of rooms in the house. The small window opposite from Judi's bed was closed. Pieces of leaves were stuck to the glass, slowly falling down as the rain came down. Judi was sleeping.

Tiptoeing over to her against my better will, the wooden floor creaked with every step. To me, she already looked dead. What was left of her gray hair was pulled back, her face skeletal, cheekbones stretching her skin. My eyes were locked on the cross above her bed.

A few minutes passed, and I left the room. A dull moan echoed through my mind as the door shut behind me. It could have been the rain, or could have been Judi. I did not want to know. When I was seven years old, Judi told my mother that I was not on the path to righteousness. She could see it in my eyes.

From that point on, I hated the fucking woman.

"Castor, how's everything going at the newspaper?" Harold had his legs crossed, sitting at the kitchen table.

"Things are great. Our readership is up a little bit, and I think it has something to do with the type of stories we're covering."

"Good to hear." He flipped his head down and took a sip of his coffee. He never looked old to me, but I could see the wear in his face. He was tired.

Gregory and J.C. were in the living room, watching an old episode of 'The Twilight Zone'. Gregory would take deep breaths and run his left hand through the blonde locks on his head. He looked uncomfortable.

J.C. was nodding off. His eyes were halfway closed. A seventeen-year-old would probably have better things to do on a Friday night than sit in a stuffy house with relatives he doesn't see often, waiting for a nun upstairs to die. I suppose I had better things to do, as well.

"Nancy, will dinner be ready soon?" Harold had finished his coffee and looked bored.

My mother didn't answer him. Dinner was eventually served, but conversation was lacking. J.C. openly asked a question about Judi, but no one answered him. Talking about Judi previous to this week was often avoided. The convent had rushed her off to us. They had avoided questions about Judi as well. She was the gray sheep of the family: people either hated her or loved her. On many occasions, she would lambaste members of the family, judging them based on their willingness to be part of the Roman Catholic faith. If you were the niece or nephew that went to church once a year, she probably hated you. I was that great nephew to her. And I heard about her disappointment in me on too many instances.

It was too fitting that we were all congregated here for her death. Her passing was imminent, and I can bet Harold and my mother felt guilty for thinking it was a type of waiting game. I had flown home for this. It wouldn't be right to leave my mother all alone with her dying aunt. It was bad enough that the church wanted nothing do with Judi's final days.

"Out of respect for her, we're going to stick together this week. All we can do is pray for her," my mother told me after dinner. "That church wanted her out of there as quickly as possible. It's horrible that they would do something like that after all of those years Judi was involved with God's work."

I wasn't sure of what exactly the doctors had told my mother, but Judi resembled a breathing corpse two floors above. Death was just around the corner, but not a single member of the family knew that it wouldn't be Judi slipping away.

It would be them.

#

It was early enough in the morning where I considered it still to be part of the night. Darkness everywhere, birds chirping, and the clank of something falling in Judi's room. My mother was the first to reach the room. Harold was tying up his bathrobe when I finally made it to the room. Rubbing sleep out of my eyes, I could see that my mother was holding the silver cross in her hand. Her eyes were teary, but she made no noise. She placed the cross back up on the wall above the bed.

"She's fine," she whispered to the room. Staring straight ahead and clutching the cross in one hand, she pulled Judi's blanket with the other, over the nun's chest and touching her chin. Gregory and J.C. never came out of the guest room to see what was going on. I didn't blame them.

It continued to rain the rest of the day, an ominous gray swooping over the house. I would learn eventually that we would never be free of its death grip. My mother was the only one who actually woke up at a normal hour. She made breakfast in the kitchen, a bandanna keeping her platinum hair out of her face. I heard her knock at my uncle's door. I lay awake, staring at the ceiling. Deep breath by deep breath, I studied the small water stains above me.

"Castor, breakfast is ready."

The droplets hit harder outside. I pulled the shade down and went downstairs. Harold poured a glass of tap water and put a neon green straw inside. "I'll take this upstairs to Judi." My mother nodded and adjusted the tie on her bandanna. Harold sighed and took off. I poured a cup of apple juice and eased into a chair. I wasn't hungry, in fact, I hadn't been since coming back to this house.

"Look at that rain out there. It just makes everything worse, doesn't it?"

I frowned in agreement and finished my juice.

"Well, I'm going to clean up here and run a few errands. The nurse should be coming by soon." My mother didn't seem enthused. "She might stick around for a bit, so make sure you offer her something to eat, Castor."

I forced a smile. "Not a problem."

About five minutes had passed and Harold returned to the kitchen. His face was more pale than previously, and his big brown eyes looked as if they wanted to jump out of the sockets and dance on the floor.

"Uncle Harold, everything okay?"

Silence.

"Is Judi alright?" The concern in my voice was surprisingly genuine.

Harold looked at me and for a moment I thought he might burst into tears. He didn't, but soon turned away and clenched his teeth.

"Harold...what's wrong? Are you sure Aunt Judi is fine?"

More silence. And then he walked away, into the living room.

"It's not right. It's not right. It's not right. It's not right," he repeated, now sitting in the purple sofa near the living room window. Pacing back and forth, he was now crying, his tears flowing. They fell onto the carpeted floor, lost forever. Something was definitely not right. And now I was wondering if Judi was still alive.

"It's not right. It's not right. It's not right. It's not right. It's not right. It's not right. It's not right." Harold held onto the mantra. His bathrobe opened a little, exposing his pot belly and hairy chest. His pudgy hands gripped the sides of his head, tugging on the hair as he wept. "It's not right. It's not right. It's not right. It's not right. It's not right."

"Harold! What is it?!"

I ran up the stairs, passing the closed guest room doors and up to the second flight, gliding two stairs at a time. The door to Judi's room was cracked open. The only light in the room was the gentle glow of spring's showers outside. Judi was sleeping. Her chest barely moved up and down. Edging closer to her, I saw the glass of water on its side by the nightstand, the neon green straw still inside. It wasn't broken, but there was a crack running through its side. I picked it up and leaned closer to Judi. There was nothing wrong with her.

Did she say something to Harold?

Back downstairs, I placed the glass on the kitchen counter, noticing the knife block next to the microwave was on its side. Peeking into the living room, Harold was no longer sitting on the sofa, but his bathrobe was on the floor, next to the ottoman. There were three rooms in the first floor of the house: the kitchen, the living room and small bathroom. Harold wasn't in any of them. I could hear him muttering when I hit the fourth step of the staircase. When I reached the second floor, I noticed the bathroom door was closed.

"It'll all come around again. We'll be judged. It'll all come around again," Harold shouted from the bathroom, his voice muffled only by the closed door.

"Harold! Open this door right now!" There were goosebumps on my arm.

"We'll be judged. It's coming."

"May God have mercy on us all." Harold was still crying.

"Harold, open the fucking door!" It was happening in slow motion. Every forceful jab of my arm seemed to take forever to follow through. Harold's voice faded away, and now I heard the wind outside gushing in. A thud came next. The sound of the wind was now the only thing I heard. Standing still for a moment, I didn't know whether to break down the door or run downstairs to call the police.

Gregory stood behind me. I don't know how long he had been behind me. "Dad! Dad! Open the door!"

We could hear the shower curtains flapping against the porcelain bathtub.

"Dad!"

I pushed Gregory out of the way and barreled into the door, forcing it open. My uncle was on his back, naked. The knife was halfway through his neck. Whatever rain that had been blown in was starting to wash away the blood, dripping onto the blue tiled floor.

Gregory knelt to the ground. "Dad...dad...d-d-d-dad..." Harold's teeth were still clenched, even in death.

It'll all come around again.

#

J.C. gripped the collar of his ruffled white t-shirt and leaned against the doorway to the living room. Gregory was sitting at the kitchen table with my mother, who held his hand, patting it. The police had just left.

"My father killed himself." J.C. was not the most emotional of any teenagers, but I knew that soon all he would want was to be in his father's arms. Losing a father is something you eventually get used to.

"He killed himself."

"I know, J.C., I know, buddy." I held onto his hand and he buried his face into my chest. "Castor, he fucking killed himself."

When I was J.C.'s age, my uncle would playfully punch me in the arm and ask me how many chicks I had slept with. My mother would yell at him. My uncle was now wrapped in a thick black bag, on his way to the morgue. The mortician is probably going to shake his head, wondering why a man would take his own life. He most likely asks these questions everyday. My family does not have to ask these questions, but now we were. And upstairs, Judi was still dying.

#

My mother was sleeping. J.C. and Gregory were packing their things. Harold's body was going to be flown back to Seattle for the wake and funeral. Gregory slipped his headphones out of his ears when I walked into the room. "Hey Castor," he sniffled. "Make sure you hook me up with a few issues of your paper. I still haven't read any of your columns."

Gregory was still in college, studying journalism. I was glad to see someone was following in those barely noticeable footsteps of mine. "Sure thing. When are you guys flying back?"

He closed his eyes. "I don't think J.C. is ready to go back home. He'll fly back tomorrow night. I have a flight in the morning."

I nodded. "Okay. Well, let me know if you need anything." Growing up without a father isn't something you get used to.

J.C. came into the room. "I think I'm going upstairs to see the old woman. Maybe seeing how she is, you know, might make me feel better. Aren't nuns supposed to have that effect?" He was a great kid, but no one ever said he was the smartest one in the family.

"She might be sleeping. And I know she hasn't said a word since coming here," I said.

J.C. shook his head. "I know. But maybe I'll just sit next to her and talk. I remember doing that when I was a kid. She was mostly mean to me, but she always listened." He went up the stairs, and I went into my room. Gregory put his headphones back in and sat down on one of the guest-room beds.

I must have fallen asleep at some point, because I woke to screaming. Nearly falling off my bed, I ran out of the room and into the hallway.

"It's coming! It's coming! It's coming!" J.C. was screaming at the top of his lungs. His t-shirt was ripped in several places, barely hanging off of him.

"J.C.! What's wrong?" Gregory was holding his brother, who jetted back and forth, trying to break free. "Tell me!"

"Greg! What the hell is going on?"

He was now holding J.C. from behind, trying to keep him down. "I...don't know! He came down after seeing...Judi! Calm down, bro!" J.C. was lunging back and forth. "He came down like this, just started screaming."

His eyes bulging and muscles pumping, J.C. was in hysterics. He broke free of his brother's grasp and ran away, practically jumping down the entire set of stairs leading to the first floor.

"It's coming! It's coming! It's coming!"

Gregory started down the stairs just before me. J.C. had already pushed the front door open. When I finally got to the bottom of the staircase, the door was flapping back and forth. The rain was relentless.

"J.C.!" Gregory was shouting, his entire body soaked.

The same feeling that crept through my body when Harold started acting crazy had now returned. I leaned against the doorway, the droplets pelting my face. Gregory was now on his knees in the driveway, screaming for his brother. He was screaming for my cousin, the quiet seventeen-year-old that did not want to spend the weekend here. The same seventeen-year-old who was now in the middle of the main road a quarter of a mile from the house, frantically waving his fists in the air, repeating the same phrase: "It's coming."

The numbness left my body and soon I was running behind Gregory, who was only a few paces ahead of me. For a miserable day, there were plenty of cars on the road, all of them swerving out of the way of J.C. Each SUV, each jeep, each sedan narrowly missing him.

"It's coming!"

"J.C.! Get out of the road! Now!" Gregory was crying. His voice cracked and sparkled in the wind.

For a second, J.C. stopped moving. He looked at his brother, then at me. J.C., the reserved teenager, his ragged shirt glued to his wet skin. With a sickening thud, a Cadillac connected with my cousin, his arms flailing forward, sending his torso and waist into a V-shape. The car skidded ahead, while J.C. toppled over and onto the side of the road. Gregory ran over to his brother. Knelt down beside him, he held his cold fingers with one hand and placed the other on his chest.

"J.C...."

His eyes now nothing but two serene white slivers, J.C.'s body thrashed as he went into shock. Gregory was silent, but his grip was strong. I stood in the rain, barely able to breathe in and out. As J.C. slipped out of this world, I turned and looked back to where we had run from. A mist had begun to circulate from the woods surrounding the road. It danced in the rain.

#

My mother extended a hand to me. My fingers locked within hers, I squeezed. "This has to be a dream. It has to be." She sighed and laid her head against my shoulder. My heart would never again feel comfortable inside my chest.

"Gregory skipped his flight. He's in the guest room. He might stay for another day or two."

All I could do was nod. All I was thinking about was the nun two floors above me, her impending death turning into parallel suffering for the rest of us. Both Harold and J.C. were gone, when it should have been her that slipped away. Both of them talked to her right before their minds turned upside down, and I wanted to know what she said to them. I wasn't a devout Catholic, but I knew strangling a nun with your bare hands would probably not sit very well with God.

My mother brushed her hair out of her eyes and kissed me on the cheek. "I'm going to check on your cousin. Castor, take a nap. Your eyes are bloodshot."

The last thing I wanted to do was sleep. "Sure, Mom."

The past three days felt like an extended dream sequence, one with rain replacing the cold sweat. One with the sting of loss at the end. Judi slept two floors above me. I glanced at the clock on the living room wall. Each second that she lived was another second that any one of us could die, and none of us knew why.

#

The rain struck the living-room window as I awoke from my unplanned nap. Yawning, I eased myself up and looked outside. Night had fallen and I was alone in the room. The light from the kitchen peeked into my vision. My mother was sitting at the table, sipping a cup of tea and reading a book. She was always the one in the family that maintained normalcy in the wake of crisis.

I couldn't help but think of Harold. Only two years away from retirement. J.C., the youngest person in the family, he was a year away from college. A year away from *starting* his life. They were both gone. And Judi was here, rotting away upstairs.

My mother smiled as I walked past her. My hand slid against her chair as I left the kitchen to check on Gregory. Gregory, who in the span of two days had lost both his father and brother. I could hear him sobbing in the guest room. I resisted the urge to knock and instead went to my own room.

The bed swallowed my body, welcoming me into its softness. If I went to sleep forever, maybe the reality of this dream would disappear. Maybe it would all go away. Tossing and turning inside the blankets, I knew that checking on Gregory was something I should have done. When I opened the door to my room, I immediately noticed that Gregory's was open. He wasn't in the guest room. The door to Judi's room slammed from above.

She's going to talk to him.

Shaking my head, I leaned against the hallway wall and slipped down. Sitting on the floor, I was only wondering what was going on between Judi and Gregory. He could be seeking her angelic solace, or she could be whispering the words of the dead into his heartbroken soul.

Ten minutes or so passed, and Gregory slowly walked down the stairs and past me. He muttered not a single word. Not a single phrase. He stared straight ahead and walked into his room, calmly closing the door behind him. I expected to hear screaming. I expected to hear shouting. Instead, I heard nothing but my own thoughts. When the tears started to form in my eyes, the thoughts disappeared. They dripped down my cheeks and into my mouth. My eyelids grew heavy, and soon they fell.

#

I could hear my mother drop the mug of coffee on the floor. She muffled her own screams as I awoke from my slumber in the hallway. She knelt against the guest-room door, crying. Forcing myself to stand up, I tried to take it all in. The scene in front of me was something I expected. Gregory's body swung from the base of the guest-room's fan. His face bloated and purple, his swelled cheeks about to burst.

My mother heaved panic breaths of air. My bare feet stuck to the wooden panels of the hallway floor. I felt a slight breeze from my cousin's swinging body. Gregory had tied the bed sheets into a long, white snake of fabric and used it as a noose. His arms dangled by his side. For some reason, I figured that once he threw himself from the bed, he didn't grab at his neck. I knelt next to my mother and held her for what felt like hours. The rain ravaged the house. Each drop emanated through our bodies. When we finally stood up, she pointed out a piece of paper crumpled in what was left of the sheets on Gregory's bed.

We will be judged. It will come. It will come soon.

Gregory's handwriting was in cursive; perfectly-spun letters detailing an unknown fate for us all. The same two paramedics who took away Harold were the ones bringing away my cousin. Their green jackets sopping wet, they walked into the guest room.

"Jesus…"

When we were kids, whenever one of us accidentally spurted "Jesus Christ" in any context other than prescribed by Judi, she'd grab the offender by the ear and twist it. One of the paramedics pulled my mother aside and gave her a small orange bottle of little blue pills. A few hours after Gregory's body was taken away, my mother finally closed the door to the guest room. When she got to her room, I imagine that she swallowed two of the Xanax and quickly fell asleep.

I spent the remainder of the night watching the rain hit the living-room window. The moonlight struck the evergreen leaves of our front yard, swaying back and forth in the light breeze of the late hours of the night. When morning hit, I woke my mother.

"I need you to stay away from Judi." Her blue eyes looked back at me, confused.

"Castor…"

"Don't go upstairs. When she dies, she dies."

She rubbed the sleep out of her eyes. "The past few days have been a nightmare, honey, I know. This entire thing feels like a dream. But it has *nothing* to do with Aunt Judi. We see Harold and his boys once or twice a year. They could have problems that we don't know about. Problems that we *shouldn't* know about."

"Mom, we've spent a week in Hell."

"We can't undo what happened, Castor. My heart is split into pieces, baby, believe me. When the nurse comes by today, we're going to find out how Judi is doing. It's a miracle she's been with us this long."

I clenched my teeth.

"You need sleep." She swung her legs over and sat up on the sofa. "I'm going to make some coffee before the nurse gets here."

She left the bottle of Xanax on the coffee table. When she left the living room, I took two and felt at home on the plush purple sofa against the window.

#

The storm continued to beat down the world outside. The church's appointed nurse rifled through the dishwasher. My head nestled in the corner of the sofa, I forced myself to drift back into consciousness. It was only a matter of seconds before I was sitting up, about to walk into the kitchen.

"Mister Hallaway, how are you?" I think her name was Betty, or Bobbi. It began with a "b," I was sure of.

"It's been a rough week."

"I know, sweetie." She pinched my cheek and smiled. Her slender finger turned my skin a light shade of pink.

Bobbi, or Betty, zipped up her leather trench coat. "I'm sure your mother was going to tell you, but...your aunt doesn't have very long left to live. Her heart rate is very low. There's nothing else we can do. She might not make it through the next 48 hours."

I nodded.

"Tell your mom I said bye, and that I'll be by in the morning."

"Where is she?"

"Your mother? She came into the room as soon as I finished up. She's been talking to Judi for the past fifteen minutes."

Talking...to Judi.

The front door slammed and my heart sank. I ran up both flights of stairs, only pausing once approaching the door to Judi's room. It took me minutes to grip the doorknob and turn it. The room was bathed in faint light coming in from the grey sky outside. The window was opened and rain was dripping in, slipping down the wall and onto the floor. My mother was curled up next to the bed, her head underneath the bed-frame. I took small steps to her, all-the-while staring at Judi, her body lain out as it had been for the past week. This past week, one of misery, one of tragedy. One of death.

As I reached the bed, I looked above Judi's dying body. The silver cross was no longer hanging from the wall. My knees cracked as I bent down to my mother. My fingers gripped the side of her arm as I pulled her closer to me. The long end of the cross was buried deep inside her eye socket, the bulbous tissue sticking to its glimmering sides. Separate trails of blood marked her face, seeping onto her white shirt and the floor below her. Long marks were embedded in the floor around her, pieces of her fingernails still stuck in the wood. There was no smile on her face, no measure of acceptance. One of her big blue eyes was gone, desecrated. A simple world of love pierced open, revealing the gloom within.

The top edge of the cross reflected in the one beam of moonlight leaking into the room. Calmly, I brushed her hair out of her face. Standing up, I pulled the chair beside the bed closer to me and sat down. It creaked as my hands brought it closer to Judi. The nun opened her eyes and I felt my spine lock, my hair standing on end. Her bony hand opened and she smiled. I placed mine into hers, and she grasped it, her cold skin enveloping mine. Judi's lips parted and the first of her words drifted out.

My mind drifted into the darkness, my soul trying to clutch its safety. Judi opened her eyes, now like little black marbles, my reflection glaring back at me. Something croaked in her throat, a long horrible creaking sound, and my reflection dissipated in a milky white cloud...and I could see it.

I could see what the others saw. Her eyes like crystal balls. Like a filmstrip of the worst day in life that hasn't happened yet.

And to know this is coming.

With a glimpse of the future in Judi's eyes, what's left of my soul, the part that hasn't withered away...the rest just gives up. Because no matter how bad giving up is, it's never been this bad. And hanging from the end of a rope doesn't sound like a bad idea. Running in front of traffic would do the trick. The only thing more heroic than suicide would be to kill everyone else before they see it too.

Because it's coming. We've felt it coming for a long time.

Thank you, Aunt Judi.

It's here.

A Quiet Desperation

Gray spots of sky, the color of purgatory. The thick air hangs around my head and for the past fifteen minutes the only thing I've wanted is to die. There was a time I thought I'd live forever, live to see the end of the world. Now, the only thing that seems concrete is the one-inch-wide bullet hole right above my spleen.

Kylee looks down at me with day-glow eyes and the look of desperation. She never wanted this. The smoke from the barrel of the gun drifts in and out of her face and I can tell that every bit of love has escaped her body.

A few raindrops hit my skin and the metallic taste in my mouth is overwhelming. The pavement below me is unquiet and comforting, the perfect place for death, the end of this pain.

The rain mixes with Kylee's anguish and the last remaining bits of sun circle around her head. Tinges of pink sky break through and I can't feel the rain anymore.

Two days ago, things were much different. Two days ago, I was a different person.

I never wanted this.

#

Tuesday gripped the edge of the chair in front of me. I could feel her eyes staring at the back of my skull, eyes that could set the controls for the heart of the sun. She was high again and it was only a matter of a few hours before she'd ask me to leave the apartment so she could cry.

I can't do this anymore, she said. I don't want my life to be like this.

Her words were shaky. On nights like this, I'd rather be buried alive than to realize I'm responsible for this beautiful girl's destruction.

I cleaned off the table with a soapy rag and caught a glimpse of myself in the small circular mirror on the kitchen counter. My face was sullen, tired. Cheeks were like pieces of latex pulled over sun-dried bone. I needed a shower, a shave and a good hour in a confession booth.

Tuesday lit a cigarette and its rosy tip inspired me to reach for the pack and light my own. Smoke billowed in my chest, the most comfortable I'd felt all night. My fingers slid across the cracked edge of the table as I searched for any excuse to keep quiet.

You have to say something at some point, Tuesday said. It's always awkward when you're here, like you're not my friend anymore.

My deep breaths responded and I sighed. I remembered the first day I first met her, the chilly autumn wind nipping at my neck, Tuesday's soft laughter as she kicked the leaves on the ground. Four years later and I'm feeding her heroin.

Britt, you should just leave, she said.

I nodded in agreement and let myself out of the apartment. The dark hallway was surprisingly inviting, the bare touch of silence and the quaint smell of apathy. Pitch black outside the window, I took another deep breath and barreled down the three sets of stairs to the lobby.

It was late November but the night wind held small traces of a warm autumn. I finished my smoke and tapped it out on the stone wall outside of Tuesday's apartment complex. If the stars were echoing the noises in her bedroom, they'd be washed with her tears, the sounds of losing a battle with herself.

Nearly forty-five minutes and a long walk back to my apartment later, I unlocked the front door and crept into the living room. Kylee was sleeping on the couch, the top half of her breasts poking out of a purple camisole tank-top. I could tell she was dreaming of me, dreaming of everything that we should have together instead of the mess that I've dragged us both into.

I gave her a light kiss on the forehead and brushed her blonde bangs out of her face. Time passed slowly when I stared at Kylee; my breaths were long and sensitive, the air between my lips as smooth as polished glass.

She had some of Tuesday's features but a person not in the know would never agree that they were sisters separated by two short years. Kylee had the qualities that made her a better person than her sister. No erratic behavior, no melodramatic instances of panic.

I poured myself a small glass of apple juice and let the plastic bottle sit halfway on the kitchen counter, just stable enough that it wouldn't fall on the floor. Kylee hated when I did that.

The two pillows on my bed were like giant puffs of heaven. My body was tired and needed to be in bed for a while. I didn't have the courage to wake Kylee and ask her to hold me, my own heart would defeat itself again after the night I just had.

Two minutes or two seconds passed and I fell asleep.

#

When I was a child, my dreams were narrow slices of black-and-white cinema. People spoke without words, their eyes obsidian drops that stained my thoughts. Not much changed as I grew up. My dreams were still black and white and the characters had the eyes of devils.

Kylee always told me that I held out my hands while I slept, looking like I was reaching for something that I could never touch.

The sun shined into my bedroom through the half-open blinds. I walked over the strands of light on the carpet and found Kylee sitting at the kitchen table, mug of coffee in one hand, the newspaper open to the arts and entertainment section. She glanced up at me and gave me the look that she had given me dozens of times before.

I know where you went last night, she said. She needs to stop,

Britt. You need to stop.

I nodded and leaned in for a kiss but she pushed me away. My heart fluttered and I clutched the kitchen counter.

Kylee, I love you, I said. Everything is going to be alright. I promise.

She shook her head and looked down at the newspaper, looked through it and through the kitchen table. Her eyes could burn a hole in the tiled floor.

If I ever knew that the two people I love the most were slowly destroying themselves, I would have killed myself a long time ago, she said.

Her bare legs were my main focus and I tried to forget that it'd been more than twelve hours since my last hit. It'd also been more than twelve hours since the last time since I was inside of Kylee. I wanted her lips on mine, her tongue tasting my body. The tears started to form in her eyes and I forced myself to leave the room. Any sound in the world wouldn't give me a jitter except crying. I'd much rather hear a saw cutting through a child's bone than hear the sad wisps of a female.

I put on my shoes and headed for the front door after grabbing the small plastic bag from my bedroom nightstand. The air was much colder than the night before and I silently wished for my leather jacket. Pounded pavement and many steps followed until I reached the alleyway between the corner Chinese restaurant and the first of five conveniences stores on this side of town.

Sitting between two steel garbage barrels and a dumpster, I pulled out the plastic bag from my pocket. The brown powder on my finger went up into my nose within a matter of seconds. The rush fell over me and I looked up at the sky. Beautiful strokes of blue above me.

The only cloud in the sky was the one above my head.

#

The first snow of the season fell onto my face, my eyelashes. It had been six hours since I left the house and at this point Kylee would have gotten tired of waiting for me to come back. Calling Tuesday would be useless; the two had a rough time talking to each other as of late.

Three elderly women walked past me on the busy street, each with department store shopping bags in their hands, genuine smiles on their faces. I wondered for a second what my life would be like without Kylee, without Tuesday.

The snow on our house looked like shimmers of glitter and I opened the front door. Kylee sat on the couch in the living room, tight black sweatpants hugging her legs, her chest hidden under a baggy beige sweatshirt. She held the gun with one hand, a beer bottle with the other.

Kylee, what are you doing, I said.

She sniffled and put the barrel to her cheek. She shook her head and cried, tears careening onto the gun, her neck. I froze and stopped breathing, then slowly walked over to her.

Honey, stop, I said. Stop it right now. Don't be fucking crazy.

Kylee looked at me, her eyes apologizing for the things I'd done wrong, the things I'd done to let her world smash into a million tiny pieces. She pulled the trigger and I stumbled back, the loveseat catching my fall. Kylee smiled and continued to cry. The gun wasn't loaded.

I wanted to, I wanted to, she said. I don't want to live like this.

My arms pulled her head into my chest and I tried not to hear the sounds of her crying. The only noises in my head were the ones I imagined, the sounds of broken guitars and the static of my mind.

You're killing yourself, she said. You're killing my sister. You're killing all of us.

I know, I said. I know.

We sat like that for two hours, on the floor. Kylee cried the entire time and my shirt sleeves were soaked by the time we stood up. She fell asleep within minutes and I lay awake the entire night, unsure of whether to remove her head from my chest or make my heart stop beating.

#

When the phone rang the next morning I knew exactly what the person on the line was going to say. It was the way the phone rang, the ringing telling its own story. The dread hit my brain, it slithered into my bones, dripping from my ribcage and everywhere below.

My father died when I was ten years old. He was a police officer, one that this town was proud to have in its ranks. He served for twenty-one years, started out working at a desk at the cramped police station, worked his way up the line. One night he left our old house for the night shift, giving me a small kiss on the forehead after wrapping my mother in an embracing hug.

Be good for your mother, he said. See you in the morning.

He walked out the door and never came back. With an hour left in his shift, he pulled over a car with a broken taillight. When my father asked the driver to step out of the vehicle, the creep pulled out a gun and shot him five times in the chest, once in the head. My mother was forced to have a closed-casket funeral.

The police eventually found the driver, a drug dealer who lived out of his '78 Buick. He sold heroin to kids from the local high school, disillusioned Goths and experimenting jocks.

It's always funny how the word "irony" can be used to describe a person's life.

I picked up the phone on the eighth ring. Fifteen seconds passed before I said anything because I knew exactly what had happened. Tuesday overdosed in her apartment. She shot up 9mg of heroin after snorting God-knows-how-much coke. Her heart stopped and apparently she died with her eyes open.

She's dead, Kylee said. She's fucking dead.

Kylee's voice always sounded much sweeter in person, her words more genuine. On the phone, she sounded surreal, like dialing zero and letting the operator tell you that your girlfriend's sister just died. Like a voiceover before the movie ends, the final words that sum up the film's theme in just a few words.

The hair on my arms stood up and I looked outside. The sun shined with uncertainty and I could smell the rain before it began to fall, the hint of death in the air. My legs refused to stand up at first, the trepidation in my chest had spread throughout my body. Even though my heart was broken, Kylee's would be much worse. She was the one who died that day, not Tuesday. Tuesday had it coming, I had it coming. Kylee was the angel, the one born to absolve our misfortunes, the one good person in our lives.

Tuesday's body would burn into ashes but it would be Kylee's that would feel the pain.

#

The raindrops hit me harder than expected. Tuesday's apartment was a long walk away, enough time for me to think of what to say to Kylee. Enough time to think my own life over before it was destroyed it even more. Scattered people passed by me on the sidewalk, each with their own destination, each walking in hurried steps and long strides. Stopping under a canopy of a small Italian restaurant, I lit a cigarette and watched a young couple at a table. The man, short black hair and sympathetic eyes, held his beau's hand, stroked it while she smiled at him. The scene gave me goosebumps.

I continued the walk to Tuesday's apartment, my soul stung and jacket sopping wet. The key in my left hand, I stood in the center of the lobby before starting up the stairs. So many times I jogged through the area in a rush. So many times that Tuesday would be waiting for me upstairs, waiting for the one thing she treasured the most.

When the heart's treasures are gone, it dies. My heart passed on a long time ago.

Kylee was most likely with her parents, so it didn't worry me to bump into her there. I walked up the stairs one-by-one, each step creaking, calling me out. It took me five minutes to reach Tuesday's door and I knocked out of habit, expecting her to quickly unhinge the locks and let me in, giving me that tight hug that I was used to.

I turned the key and opened the door, the sweet waft of oak moss and regret. So many times the soft light of the hallway lamp was turned on when I came in. Tuesday was afraid of the dark, afraid of what would happen to her if she was left alone with the absence of light.

The one time I slipped was in this hallway. My body couldn't resist Tuesday and we both gave in and added another notch to our belt of sins. The hundreds of times I made love to Kylee I was thinking of the one night that I was with her sister.

The illumination of Tuesday's past in my vision, I sat on the floor of the kitchen. This kitchen, the one where too many times I forced her to give in to her addictions, too many times I gave in to my own.

The world is only what I had made of it, a self-mocking spiral of disgust. It was only a matter of time before Kylee left me. Only a matter of time before she realized that she was dealt a bad hand.

I fumbled through the magazines on the kitchen counter and pictured a strung-out Tuesday trying to read them all at once, trying to pardon the feeling in her chest. Her bedroom door was open and I found myself sitting with my back to the bed. The first of my tears came easily. The rain outside was unforgiving and I knew that I couldn't stay in this room forever. Legs stood up when my face was dry, my body starting to feel warm again. I smoked three cigarettes and left the apartment, looking back before heading down the staircase.

Bye Tuesday, I said.

My fingers clenched the small bag of brown powder in my pocket. I picked it out and tossed it into the garbage can next to the doorway. Outside of the apartment complex, I stood for a minute and closed my eyes. Tuesday's ghost walked past me and into traffic, then she floated away. The colors of the sky bled before me, the hum of rain in the background.

#

The whine of cars screamed past me as I approached the house. The rain was steady, rampant. A breeze of violent, burnt wind at my back. The lonely white of the wooden fence in front of me.

It was only when I took my first step inside the house when the sound of a gun clicking caught me. Kylee was pointing it at me, tears hurriedly falling from her eyes. She looked beautiful, my love with a gun. My love with the intent of putting a bullet anywhere it would kill me.

You killed her, she said.

All I could do was shake my head. This life was a tragedy, a disaster. I slid off my jacket, my soaked t-shirt exposed.

Kylee, I wasn't there, I said. I didn't know she was going to do that.

She shook her head twice, then closed her eyes. She probably thought about the time I carried her into our bedroom, only stopping to remove our clothes. Or the first time I kissed her. Or she thought about her sister, that one that I killed.

Kylee, I love you, I said. Put down the gun and let's go inside.

She shook her head again. And then fired.

#

The sky opens up and my body feels warm. My wet t-shirt burns my skin. Clumps of clouds break apart, the rain stops. The sun looks like it's dying, an orange glow fading into pink. Kylee stands over me, the gun still in her hand. I'll never have the chance to ask her to marry me, never have the opportunity to fall in love all over again.

My home is blurred in the corner of my eye. The dry and cool air cycling inside, a place that Kylee will go once my eyes close, once I stop breathing. I can't think of my family right now, I have no recollection of my mother, my father. My memory lies within the house thirteen feet away from my body.

Home is where my memory is and my memory is bleeding to death.

Midnight Souls

She moves like a crimson ghost. Every motion flutters with the glittery viscera of a million shimmering butterflies. Hair as black as ash swims in a sea of endless auburn and for the fifteen seconds it takes her to saw through the nameless man's arm I'm sure I've never loved anyone as much as her. A crimson geyser sprays plasma the color of broken rubies and a single miscible scream penetrates the layers of the dank hotel room, lost somewhere between the moon and the stars.

Penny takes a breath and sits at the edge of the bed, the weight of our world pressing into her shoulders like an angel's fists. The man falls forward, clasps the fresh stump with white-knuckled fingers, and softly moans until a thin layer of saliva escapes his lips and collects into a mirrored pool on the carpet.

I stand up, dig my soul out of chest and kiss Penny's forehead. A trail of comet dust spins between our bodies when she looks down at the unconscious man. I collect the thirteen-inch blade from the center of the bed and wipe it clean with a beige hand-towel. Penny crosses her legs and removes the small makeup container from her purse on the side of the bed. She checks her eyeshadow, blinks three times, and smiles with cheeks the color of Christmas morning.

The man squirms beneath me and when I place a pillow under his head, he looks at me with eyes of desperate abandon. Neither of us knew his real name and he paid the full three thousand in crisp, unmarked cash that was housed in a briefcase that smelled of whiskey and regret. Penny reaches over for the phone on the mahogany nightstand and hits the button to reach the front desk.

"There's been an accident in room 217," she says, and leaves the receiver disconnected to hang from the side of the night-stand. She takes my hand, immediate warmth and comfort spinning in my veins like fiery heroin, brings her lips to mine.

I grip the small of her back and bring her body closer to mine, dewy lavender scent of her tingling the edge of my nose. "Let's get out of here," I say.

She smiles and nods, blush of her dimples radiating the dark light streaming from the silent black-and-white television in the corner of the room. We walk past the dead limb separated from its host and as I flip the duffel bag over my shoulder, I silently hope that I forget the momentary look on our client's sodden face as he awakes from the foggy nightmare of a dry October evening.

#

Penny sips her wine as if she's never had a glass before this evening. She licks her lips every few seconds as if to savor the years the liquid lived in the opaque green bottle. "You've never wondered what it feels like? What it means to experience it?"

I shake my head, down another gulp of Guinness. "Not for a second."

It's when she smiles that I picture the first time we met. The balsam forest-green of her eyes twinkles with stray moonlight and for a moment I'm a child again. "I can't believe that for a second," she says. "After all we've done together, you must want to know what lies on that other side, you know, the words and thoughts and visions they all claim to have after we're done."

Another long sip of beer, another cool burst of autumn wind from the open window in the corner of our kitchen. "No. I can't. I never have, Penny, and I never will."

She sighs and finishes the glass of wine, downing the swirling purple remnants with a final swish of her tongue. She stares out into the midnight sky. "That man tonight, when he had called, it was almost as if he believed everything he heard. How he could one day see *them*, the ones all around us."

It's right here that I stop drinking, grit my teeth together with the force of a thousand wild boars. I've heard it all before, the talk of their shadows, the way they dance in the empty matter floating above and below us within every step we take. The truth is that I don't want to know what's living next to me. The truth is that the amount of pain experienced in one of our sessions isn't enough for me to believe that there's more to this existence than the physical world around us.

Penny's cell phone rings and the warmth inside my chest dissipates into a broken silhouette against the celluloid behind my eyes.

#

His name, he says, is Kleyton Parker. Red leather cowboy boots, black jeans and an arrogant smile. His eyes slink back-and-forth as if they're baby black garden snakes. He sits in the hotel bar and sips on a clear martini. Every few seconds he checks out Penny's cleavage and makes it hard for me to forget that he handed us just over five grand in cash just ten minutes ago.

"You're a lucky guy, muchacho." A wink and another gulp of his drink. I nod politely. "Yeah."

I can tell Penny's getting anxious because she slides a black-painted fingernail against the edge of her glass, the other hand reflecting through the liquid like a patch of baby black widows. She looks at the neon orange clock above the bar and nods at me. "Let's get this started," she says, and picks up her purse.

"You guys don't want another drink? It's on me." Kleyton stands up from the bar and raises his glass to the air.

"No thanks. What room number are you in?"

He downs the last of his drink. "Two seventeen."

Penny leads the way and Kleyton and I follow her directly into hell.

#

The radiance of a dozen shattered rays of moonlight pierces the open hotel room air like a rainstorm of silver knives. Penny drops her oversized purse on the edge of the pine desk and fishes out a syringe and two small bottles. I pour myself a scotch from the bar in the corner of the room. Kleyton smiles as I drop an ice cube into my glass.

"I see it's your lady that does all of the heavy lifting." A sharp chuckle and he leans against the window, facing my wife. "It's okay, though. I like me a lady that's a hard worker."

Penny draws a few milliliters of morphine from the first bottle and sprays the tip of the needle into the air. "I need you to sit down over there and be quiet."

Kleyton raises his arms up and scoots over to the other side of the room. He sits in the armchair next to the bar. "Don't worry, little lady. I promise not to squirm."

"Good, because that's a fantastic way of making this a lot worse than it could be."

I finish my scotch in two large gulps and place the glass at the edge of the bar, halfway on the edge of the pine and halfway into the rest of the room. I've done it enough times to know that if the glass falls, the evening won't go as quickly as I'd like it to. Kleyton fidgets his fingers on the arms of his chair as Penny pulls up the sleeve of his designer flannel shirt. A crow on the edge of the windowsill catches my attention and in the ten seconds that its eyes dance with mine a sharp shriek pricks the calm, dewy air.

The next black shape I see is a gun. Kleyton jams the weapon in my face and in a quick swirl swipes it across my cheek. The pain is nothing compared to seeing a near-stranger with his arm around my wife's neck.

"Don't fucking move," he says, pulls Penny to the other side of the room.

I wipe the blood from my face and taste the rust of rage against the tip of my mouth. "Let her go."

Kleyton laughs, pulls the side of Penny's hair so hard that I can see the hurt in her rosy cheeks. "I don't know how many of these the two of you have done, but along the way, something like this was bound to happen."

"We'll give you our money, Kleyton. Just, please, let her go."

He shakes his head, holds my wife tighter against him. "It's not about the money, cowboy. Believe me, if I was short on cash, I would have never been able to pay that God-awful deposit the two of you required for this here visit. What I'm here for isn't something you can give." He pauses for a second and I swear his shadow dances in the moonlight. "I promise this will be quick."

What happens next occurs in blocky, blurry shapes that radiate with a prismatic glow. A jumbling arrangement of sharp noises and metallic whirls spin in my head like a broken symphony. I ignore the tinges of pain beneath my skull and lunge at Kleyton but I'm greeted with a jagged whip of the pistol butt. Blood spools out of my mouth like a jagged spider web and when the first of Penny's screams pierces the air, I can't tell if I'm alive or dead.

Fade into white and back to grey. Ten seconds or ten days passes and she's lying next to me, her right hand on my chest and clenching my shirt with cherry-stained fingers. The other hand sits ten feet from her body. Kleyton backs away from the scene until his boots scrape across the floor and hit the edge of the opposite wall.

Penny's fingers release the fabric of my t-shirt and she lies motionless and pale. She rolls over to her backside and pushes her body away from me and into the corner between the bar and the window. Her eyes are as black and dead as a newborn demon's and a comet streak of albino white dresses her once auburn locks. She pays no attention to the blood escaping from her new wound.

"Look at her hair…" Kleyton's lips nearly swallow his entire face. "Jesus."

Kleyton grabs the doorknob and struggles to swing it open.

My last sight of him is the serene wrinkle in his forehead, the two morose eyes locked onto my wife as if his actions changed all of our lives.

I stare at the various stains on the hotel room ceiling and within seconds our shadows have collected our consciousness and dropped us into a frozen slumber.

#

You were barely seventeen and perfect. Lips of an angel, dimples that could hold a man's soul. You held my hand during the rainstorm and pointed at every shooting star, leaning in for kisses whenever there was a gap in time and space. You smelled of lavender and an autumn afternoon, skeletons of leaves as brown as dead pumpkins.

"Look," you said, and pointed to a fiery trail in the October night sky.

I gazed above and when my eyes were ablaze with the reflections of glitter and hail you pressed your mouth against mine and sucked the memories from the back of my throat and swallowed them. Your eyes shifted from blue to gray and back again.

Our fingers entwined, alpine purple nails trailing the edges of my palms, we let the rain beat down upon our hearts as if nothing could ever stop us.

#

Penny's eyes draft from side-to-side as if she's following a tennis match. I hold her hand in mind but it's been at least a week since she last squeezed back. Her breaths are consistent and slow. The white steak in her hair remains cold, a reminder of the events before us. Every few hours she smiles and points behind me.

"They're right behind you," she says. "Red eyes like fire. They're all around us, baby. I don't think you should be scared."

I can't turn around, can't bear to think of her this way

anymore. I kiss the back of her hand, remember the days when we'd watch the geese in the Charles River and drink coffee and follow the moon back home.

Another kiss on her forehead but she doesn't look directly at me. She keeps pointing to the empty hospital sky. I leave her behind me when the night beckons and walk to the only place in Boston where the one person I need to see could possibly be.

#

I spot him walking in through the front lobby. Eleven hotels on this strip of downtown and I was bound to be lucky. I keep a distance from his back, careful not to let my reflection catch the rugged look he still wears on his face. He sips a beer at the bar across from the lobby and it's only a few minutes into his first drink that his client walks over and sits across from him. I study the client's mannerisms, the nervous twitch at the tips of his sneakers, the wavy cowlick that shoots into the sky with an awkward sway. I wait another ten minutes for them to get the small talk out of the way before I get up from the velvet couch in the lobby.

Kleyton walks away first and the man follows suit within the next eighty seconds. I walk quickly until I reach the set of elevators near the bar. Kleyton is smart and gets on the first elevator but lets the man catch the next one. We're the only two in the next ride and when he pushes the 'four' button a bright hurried pinch of light escapes from the metal panel.

We reach the fourth floor and he exits first. A quick scan of the hallway shows there's no one else breathing here except for us. It happens almost too quickly and when his windpipe slams against my knuckles it sounds like a popping soda can. I toss aside his cash and license and credit cards but instead grab the key ring from his inside jacket pocket and catch the momentary trance of golden light from the '423' on the ring.

The room's only a minute's walk away from the elevator. I knock once for each time my heart beats through my ribcage.

"Thanks for waiting a few minutes to—"

Kleyton can barely finish his sentence before I shove my weight through the door and onto his chest. For a man that's only a decade or so older than me he's not nearly as strong as I'd imagined. He gasps for air in between my fist cracking the side of his head. When he stops moving I slam the door shut behind me and smile.

#

Kleyton's eyelids swing open. The fear in his pupils dances behind the sweat and blood that have caked into his sockets.

"What...the fuck?" Only three words from a man who, with our situations reversed, wouldn't be able to shut up.

"The quieter you are, the less this will hurt." I only had to fish through his duffel bag for a few seconds before finding the polished cleaver.

Kleyton's eyes follow the moonlight's reflection off the knife and a single swift blow to his jaw is enough to rattle him one last time. He stops squirming when the cleaver hits the open air and corrals into the flesh. It takes three swipes to cut through completely and Kleyton is silent as soon as the forearm is split from the wrist and hand on his right side. Lips part open so wide that they could swallow himself and the chair he's sitting in.

"So...beautiful..." Tinny strands of fresh saliva fall from his mouth and onto his lap. "In the air, behind the bed, all around us..."

I launch the cleaver against the side of the desk on the opposite side of the room. Telephone off the hook and Kleyton bleeding out, I nod at the scene and leave the room and the hotel as fast as a ghost falling from the heavens.

#

Another shot of tequila with no chaser. I stare at a butcher knife Penny used to use on our clients. The wooden handle is beaten and raw. I'm surprised the splinters never found their way into her palm. I finish the rest of the tequila and move onto the half-empty bottle of whiskey across the table in our kitchen. Penny's asleep in the bedroom but nowadays slumber to her isn't really rest at all. She says they talk to her when her eyes are closed. They tell her about what's beyond the arc of this world and the next.

I toss my black t-shirt onto the kitchen floor, feel the cool breeze of an October evening across my bare chest. I stretch my fingers, crack the knuckles with a deep breath. Eyes closed, I grip the knife, let it sway over my wrist before swallowing the last mouthful of whiskey. I let it fall with a resounding screech and picture Penny's face in the moonlight, her smile as soft as a seraph's voice.

The first one skitters from the corner of the kitchen and over my head. The next one sniffs the new wound, its horns and oval head shifting from side-to-side with a magnetic swing. One of them walks into the kitchen, a pure obsidian form nearly blanketed by dark light. Its eyes glisten with a scarlet glow.

A Thousand Black Flowers

Will watched a long puffy string of clove smoke drift into the endless glitter of moonlight. He blocked out the muddled voices circling around him and tried to think of all the joyful moments that had encompassed his sister's life. When the coroner zipped her up only a dozen feet away, Will swore that the sounds of rusted metal locking together were the only things he would hear for the rest of his life. He stamped out the cigarette on the apartment steps and sighed, range of shock still at the tip of his brain. The dirty orange glow from two jack o' lanterns on the porch of the house where Sonia just killed herself reflected off the pale blue of his tired eyes.

It took Will a few minutes to let everything settle in. He was dozing off on the couch around midnight when his cell phone beeped. He rubbed the beginnings of sleep out of his eyes and stared at the screen, pupils struggling to read a text from Sonia. The haze of slumber fighting his vision for control of his mind, he scanned the two words on the screen: *Save me.* With no return after a half dozen calls to her line, Will threw on his jacket and started to drive to her house. It was only when the Taunton Police Department called him a half hour ago did his night take an unanticipated turn.

Now Will stood in the front of the house in which he and Sonia had grown up. His sister had been inside their childhood home and threw herself to her own death three floors below, and the police couldn't pinpoint a motive. Will reached into his pocket and fetched the crumpled pack of European cigarettes. Slender black funnel of tobacco between his lips, he lit its tip and took a comforting drag.

"Mr. Dawson?"

Will spun around and faced a man wearing beige khakis and a navy blue blazer. The man outstretched a hand and smiled. "I'm

Detective Brady," he said.

Will nodded and ignored the handshake. "What happened to my sister?"

Detective Brady sighed, rosy red cheeks flush with an autumn breeze. "I'm sorry for your loss. We're doing everything we can. I don't know how long you lived in this town, but today and tonight are pretty busy for us, Halloween and all. You know?" Brady looked around and pointed at the array of seasonal directions garnering the neighborhood of homes. "I'm going to have a couple of my guys follow through with this. We're going to find out why your sister did what she did...I promise."

Will watched the sparkle in Brady's eyes and could tell that the detective was sincere in his words. "Thanks. My sister sent me a text. I only wished I could have gotten to her in time. I was on my way to her house when you guys called."

Brady tilted his head. "What time was this?"

"A little after midnight, I think. It said *save me*." Will forced himself to hold back a stream of tears. He didn't know why the emotions were trapped for so long and were beginning to find their way out now. He bit his bottom lip and focused on the minute bit of pain. "I can't believe she's dead..."

Brady placed a hand on Will's shoulder. "I'm sorry, Mr. Dawson. Please go home and get some rest." He handed Will a creased business card. "Please call me first thing in the morning. We're going to try and retrace your sister's steps. There must have been something that forced her to do this."

"Thanks." Will shoved the card in his front jeans pocket and walked away. He wiped the corners of his eyes and savored a long drag of the cigarette.

#

Will sat at the kitchen table and threw back another shot of whiskey. Before he could fill the glass again, three sharp raps filled the room and he realized someone was knocking. He jogged to the other side of the apartment and opened the front door.

"Will…"

The unmistakable crux in Jake's voice nearly elicited another set of tears. Sonia's boyfriend stood in the open doorframe, bags under his eyes like signs of lost love. Will embraced the man in his arms with an immediate hug. "I can't believe this is happening."

Will backed away and motioned for Jake to follow him into the house. "I know, Jake. I'm sorry."

Jake sat on the lone living room sofa and immediately rested his head back. "Is this what shock feels like, Will? I feel like I shouldn't be able to walk, or talk, or – "

"It's shock, Jake. It'll fade soon. What were you guys doing last night?"

Jake pouted his lips in thought. "We had dinner around nine, I think. We had met at the Sundown Pub right after work, and after we ate she got a phone call from Judy, this chick that she works with. They've been going to these Reiki sessions on the other side of Taunton."

"You mean that Japanese spiritual therapy thing?" Will couldn't remember Sonia mentioning anything about it.

"Yeah." Jake fiddled with his thumbs, eyes glued to a blank television screen. "Listen, Will, there's something I need to tell you."

Will perked up and found himself standing above Jake, ready to burst into a fit of anger at any moment. Although he was positive that the two never kept secrets from him, his sister's suicide had quickly taught him that not all was what it had seemed. "What is it, Jake?"

Jake threw his arms in the air. "Sonia had a miscarriage last month."

The word itself –miscarriage– sent a shiver of abandon

through Will's spine. He sat down next to Jake and took a deep breath. To think that his sister was pregnant and lost a baby shattered his already broken heart. "I'm sorry, Jake," was all Will could muster.

Jake's eyes began to water. "She was strong through it all, Will. So fucking strong. I kept telling her that we'd try again someday, but eventually it wore down on her. She went to three different therapists and not a single one of them could help. The pain...you could see it in her eyes, Will."

Will nodded.

"She tried everything to get over it. She took tabs of Xanax, Ambien, anything to help her get through the night. But nothing worked, Will. *Nothing*. And this woman Judy at her office told her about Reiki practitioners, this type of spiritual therapy that would be able to heal her for *good*."

"Where is this place?" Will noticed the apprehensive tone of his voice.

Jake stood up and looked out the window. An array of orange lights hung from a neighboring building. "I think it's near Jamison Road, the west side of Taunton."

Will looked at his watch and noticed that it was only five in the morning, even though it felt like he'd been awake for a week straight. "I bet they're not open this early. Do you have Judy's number?"

Jake nodded. "Yeah, it's in my cell phone."

Will unzipped his sweatshirt and tossed it on the back of the sofa. "Go to my room and lie down for a few hours. I'll sprawl out here. We're going to this Reiki place when we wake up, Jake. My sister was stronger than that. She would never take her own life in the midst of losing hope."

"I know, Will. I know."

Will kicked off his boots. "Get some sleep."

#

Jake took another sip of coffee, foam bubbling at the top of the cup like angry lava. "This town really goes all out for Halloween, eh?"

Will switched hands on the steering wheel, eyes focused on the road ahead. They pulled up to a red light and for a moment he could feel the spirit of the holiday in the air. A large foam pumpkin with charcoal eyes dressed the lawn of an antique store; outlines of sparkling witches adorned a nearby candy store. "That they do, Jake," he said.

When they reached Jamison Road, Will was forced to circle around the square twice before finding a parking spot. "Goddamn town fair's coming," he said aloud. "No place to park." Will slid the car into front of Deb's *Watch and Jewelry Repair*, a building that looked like it could have been a rundown bank in the early twentieth century.

Jake stepped out of the vehicle and dumped the remains of the coffee on the street. The liquid slithered into a pile of leaves. Will was about to shove the car keys into his pocket when he heard his companion shout. He quickly slammed shut the driver's side door and ran to where Jake was.

"Jake! Jake! What is it?"

Jake was already a dozen paces ahead of him. Will found himself struggling to keep up, heart racing to a frantic tune. Out of breath and sweat seeping from his brow, he reached Jake and immediately realized why his dead sister's boyfriend and future husband had started to shout.

Jake knelt next to Sonia's crimson Mustang, his pale hands running along the lone white stripe that clad its shiny exterior. "Sonia," he whispered to himself, the words floating above him and soon lost in the gentle October wind.

Will knelt beside him and they remained silent for a few moments. Will finally stood up and grabbed Jake by the arm of his olive-colored jacket. "What the hell is her car doing here?"

Rage appearing in the crevasses of his face, Jake shook his

head and ran a finger along the dirty driver's side window. Both peered into the car, hoping to find some bit of evidence that could back up Sonia's daring suicide. Will took a chance and slid his fingers under the door handle and in a matter of moments it swung open. Jake's eyes lit up with hope, and he quickly hopped into the driver's side seat. After a few minutes of rifling through Sonia's personal items, he threw his hands up in frustration and shook his head.

"Nothing," he said, eyes staring straight ahead. "Nothing."

Will nodded and the two took long strides along the sidewalk. They couldn't help but smile at the joyous faces of the young that were thoroughly enjoying the one day where makeup and masks were normality. October wind beating at their backs, they faced the front door of *Your Reiki: Spiritual Therapy for the Soul*. Located in a suburban home rather than a business building, Will studied the exterior of the house and noticed that it looked more residential than anything else on the block.

Jake knocked on the front door twice. "This place better have answers for us," he said.

While they waited, Will lit the last cigarette in his pack. Inhaling the dewy aroma of new tobacco, he took a long drag and closed his eyes. "Has Judy called you back yet?"

Jake shook his head and knocked on the door again. "Nope. Three voicemails and a few text messages, still nothing. Goddamn it, where the hell are these people? It's nine thirty in the morning. They should be open. I'm going to – "

At his final word, the door popped open, the jingling of classic store bells ringing overhead. A woman no more than five feet tall opened the door, her hair the color of winter ash. Her face devoid of emotion, she waved in the two and pointed them to a purple sofa in the corner of the lobby. A pregnant woman opened the door and the bells startled Will and Jake.

"Hi Maria," the old woman said to her new guest. Maria nodded once, face like pastel stone, and walked up the single set of stairs across the way. She took each step in the same amount of time, as if she were robotic.

Will noticed that the room was lacking the same holiday décor that graced the rest of the town. "Not much into Halloween, are you?" Will asked.

The old woman ignored his question, her eyes blazing with a tint of orange and blue. "How can I help you guys? I'm afraid I'm all booked up for today, but if you – "

"My sister came in here last night with one of her friends." Will wasted no time in getting to the point.

"Lots of women come to visit – "

"And then she killed herself." Will didn't notice that he was only a few inches away from the woman's face. He could smell the faint aroma of plumeria and wax candles.

The woman grinned. "I have no time for Halloween pranks, young man. Please, either make an appointment or leave."

Jake hopped from the sofa and slammed his fist to the glass counter on which the woman's shoulders casually rested. "What happened to my girlfriend, old woman? Tell us!"

The old woman seemed unfounded by the irritation in Jake's voice. She lost the slight smile on her face and pulled out a large, leather appointment book from under the counter. "What was her name?" Shades of perfect white teeth peeked from her mouth, shades of black lipstick dressing her lips.

"Sonia Morris," Will said, pulling back the infuriated Jake.

The woman traced each line of the book, long black fingernails searching for the correct name. "Ah, Sonia," she said. "Lots of powerful life force in that woman. Very, very strong demeanor."

"She's fucking dead, you hag." Jake pushed away Will and was soon in the old woman's face. "This is the last place she came before she walked off the top floor of her childhood home. What did you do to her?"

"I have a name, young man. You can call me Kyllard," she said, undeterred by Jake's anger. "And I'm sorry for your loss, my friend, but all we do here is help people heal themselves by channeling the energy within."

Jake grunted and walked away.

Will stepped in and raised a hand. "Did she say anything before she left? Anything that might make you think that she'd soon commit suicide?"

Kyllard shook her head. "Not a thing."

"Let's go, Jake." Will grabbed him by the arm and pushed open the door. The bells made him want to scratch out his eyes. When the two were outside, Jake kicked a nearby trash barrel. It nearly toppled over but Will forced it back upwards to avoid causing a scene and making a mess. He cupped Jake's head in his hands and gazed deeply into his eyes. "Calm down, Jake. I'm just as hurt, sad and frustrated as you. My sister is dead. *Dead.* We will find out why she did this, but I need you to calm down."

"Okay" was the only word Jake could assemble before erupting into a full torrent of tears. Will hugged him for a few seconds and tried to ignore the sound of fresh drops of emotion hitting the ground. As he let go, Jake's cell phone rang.

"Hello?" Jake was barely able to let out a welcoming tone.

Will heard the first part of Jake's phone conversation but soon lost the statements as a female scream sliced the Halloween air. He turned around to see a woman clutching her child, who was dressed in a tiny, bright orange pumpkin outfit. The child's intense blonde hair stuck out in curls of green pipe cleaners, like the tip top of a fresh pumpkin. She pointed up at the sky and shrieked again. Will could see the outline of a figure on the roof of the house he had just left. Squinting in the light of the October sun, he barely recognized the shape as the pregnant woman who had just entered the Reiki practice. She stood at the very edge of the roof, tips of her ruby red flats curling over the landing. In a silent motion, she leaned forward and toppled into the air, body carousing downward until it struck the concrete driveway.

Bits of bone and skull erupted from the impact, strips of pink flesh plopped across the nearby grass. Will winced and turned away just as Jake walked into him. The two collided and as he caught the supple glow of Jake's tender eyes, Will vomited a stream of brown fluid on the ground. Head warm with fright, he pointed to the pregnant woman's lifeless body before a row of steel-colored clouds covered the defenseless sun.

#

Detective Brady shrugged his shoulders. Will couldn't read their lips or make out the conversation between Jake and the detective. Jake soon walked away from the detective and Will immediately noticed the nervous twitch in his eye. Jake started to speak but instead curled his lips inward. He looked up, then away, before talking. "Will...Sonia's friend Judy is dead. It was a...suicide."

Suicide. The word reached into Will's lungs and clutched gentle breaths. Will felt dizzy and sat down in the open driver's side of his car. "Jesus," he said.

"I told Detective Brady that all three of these girls were at the Reiki practice before they died. They're doing a search right now and questioning Kyllard."

Will bit his bottom lip. "They won't find anything."

"Why do you say that?"

"Something's going on in there, Jake. And our little simple police department isn't going to figure it out on their own." Will threw back the towel that the police had covered him with and ground his teeth.

"What are *we* going to do, Will? We don't even know for sure that Kyllard is causing those women to kill themselves."

Will stuck a finger in Jake's chest. "Say that again and think of your dead girlfriend. Say that again and think of my *dead sister.*"

Jake backed away and curled his fingers into two meaty fists. He bowed his head and spit on the ground.

"Exactly," said Will. "We'll wait until the police are done over there."

Jake bit the tip of his thumb. "And then what?"

"And then *we* go in."

#

Will took a long sip of beer from the bottle and stuck it between his legs in the front seat of his car. Jake leaned his head against the passenger's side window and from a distance, watched the final Taunton police officer leave the Reiki practice. He could barely see Kyllard smiling with glee, waving at the officer as he walked to his cruiser. The overweight man waved back and heaved himself into the car. He slowly backed out of the driveway and drove into the night.

Finishing his beer, Will flung the bottle into the backseat and looked out his window. "Another Halloween come and gone," he said aloud.

Jake nodded and poked at the windshield. "About time?" he asked. "The place looks empty, Will. And I can't see any more officers swarming the house."

"Let's go." Will waited for Jake to step out of the car before he locked the doors. The clinching of the locks sounded like a closing casket. Will opened the trunk and pulled out a wooden baseball bat. Jake reached into the trunk, and after tossing aside old books, videotapes and clothing, he found a rusted crowbar. Holding it in his hands, he closed his fingers around the cold metal. He nodded at Will and the two took quick strides towards the house. Crouching behind a row of bushes in the neighboring home, Will leaned into Jake and whispered. "I'll knock, and make sure you hide that crowbar. When she lets us in, we're going to force her to let us take our *own* look at the house."

"Sounds good," Jake whispered back.

Will jogged to the front door and knocked twice, baseball bat hidden behind his legs. Jake hid to the side of the door and out of sight. Kyllard pulled open the shades and shook her head in disgust. Will could tell that she was cursing. She finally opened the door a few inches, long silver hair hanging well below her shoulders.

"What do *you* want? The police just left here and found *nothing*, young man. The woman today had a lot of issues going on. We couldn't help her and she took her own steps to end her life. That's what I told the police, and that's what I'm telling you."

Will held up a hand. "Five minutes is all I want. Just to talk. Please, for my sister."

Kyllard tilted her head back. "Fine," she said, opening the door. "Five minutes and no more."

As soon as there was enough room, Will pushed her down and Jake erupted from his hiding spot. He slammed shut the door and twisted the two locks above the handle. He pulled down the shades and held out the crowbar.

"We're going to take our own look, you goddamn hag. Stay right there and don't fucking move." Jake held the tip of the crowbar to her face, but not a single shred of fear was evident on her wrinkled skin.

Will searched behind the counter and found a variety of oils, rubs and pamphlets. He pushed them all to the side and they tumbled onto the carpeted floor.

"Young man! Be respectful of my store!" She turned to Jake. "*You* will be the first, my friend."

Jake pushed the crowbar further into her face. "Yeah, okay."

"Calm down, Jake." Will hopped over the counter and back into the lobby. Only a single light bulb hanging in the center of the room provided them with dull light. He held the baseball bat to the side of her head. "We're not here to hurt you, Kyllard. We just want to look around. Jake, you go upstairs first. I'll stay here with her."

Before Jake could walk up the stairs, a dark shape entered the room from beneath the staircase. Will stood back and raised the bat. The figure wore a pure white mask, murky drops of green protruding from two shadowy eyeholes. It was draped from head-to-toe in a black velvet shawl. It grabbed Jake by the throat and in one quick swab knocked him to the ground. The crowbar flew from his hands and landed against the wall. Kyllard pointed at Will and the figure ambled over to him, arms outstretched. Will took a swing with the bat but the shape was too swift and strong; with one slap Will felt the searing sting of pain across his cheeks.

Kyllard stood and brushed herself off. "Get them upstairs."

The last thing Will saw was the infinite dark of the figure's eyes and a drop of moonlight fighting with the dreary glow of a single light bulb.

#

Will opened his eyes, the sweat of a dying dream slipping onto his nose and cheeks. He couldn't figure out where he was or what happened to him. A coverlet of orange radiance filled the room. Four or five large jack o' lanterns, black candles blazing inside, decorated the corners of the room. He looked down to see his arms and legs tied to a brown, polished rocking chair.

"Awake now, aren't we?" The haggard female voice shocked him into full awareness, and he realized where he was.

Kyllard.

Will spit a long strand of blood from his mouth and it dangled on his chin like a crimson spider web. When he saw the display in the center of the room, every bit of bile in his stomach rose to his throat. Three figures lay quietly on a glass table, each body completely devoid of skin, revealing a thick layer of wet, moving muscle. Their chests heaved in and out with gentle motions.

They're alive, Will thought.

"The life force," Kyllard said, "it keeps them *alive*, young man." She laughed a maniacal chuckle and lifted Will's chin with a single, bony finger. "Your sister, those girls, they were all *full* of it, my friend. And now their souls, their energy, are keeping my family alive."

"Alive? What are those things?" Will could hear the angry pinch of terror in his voice.

Kyllard chuckled and pointed to the body in the middle. Its lips remained open, spots of drool dressing its shiny face. "No one dies in my family, young man. *No one.*"

Will tried not to look at Kyllard's face and instead moved his head to the right. Jake sat cross-legged near the table of bodies, drool escaping his lips and dripping onto his chest. "I see it. I see it. I see it," he repeated, his voice sullen and wavy.

"Oh my God!" Will screamed. "What did you do to him? And what the hell are those things?"

Kyllard walked over to Jake and patted him on the head, emaciated hand pushing down his thick black hair like he was a tired dog. "My boy, what do you see?" Her voice was different now, and Will could hear the evil crisp in her tone.

Will felt the force of desperation grip his entire body, each fiber of every muscle struggling to break free of the horrid scene playing out in front of him. Jake stood up, his eyes now two black slits with red drops in the center. He calmly shuffled over to Will like he didn't recognize him as his future brother-in-law. Instead, Jake angled his head in confusion, soft dark bangs hanging over his forehead. He leaned in front of Jake and smiled, salivating at the tips of his lips like a frightened child. He stared at Jake for a solid minute before Will heaved himself over, chair falling to the ground. The impact of his head against the wooden floor wasn't as painful as the anticipation of death.

Kyllard shook her head. "Now, now. It's not going to do you any good to try and leave." She motioned for the large man that only a short while ago cracked his fist against Will's unsuspecting skull. The husky man, still draped in black with a mask covering his face, picked up Will by his chest and forced the chair back to its original position.

"What is wrong with you people?" The weight of Will's words did nothing to sway the mood of the ceremony in front of him.

Kyllard knelt in front of him and licked her top lip, tongue slithering over faint orange lipstick. "These beings, they're my family," she said, pointing to the line of degloved bodies in the center of the room. "We're keeping them alive. Pretty soon that warming glow in your heart is going to be given to them so they can spend more time on this earth."

"No! No!" Will attempted to force his arms upward and break the thick rope holding his wrists to the chair, but they were tied without escape in mind. He sent shocks of frantic breaths through gritted teeth.

"I can see it now," said Jake. "I can see it now. I can see it now." He repeated the phrase until it was tattooed on the walls of Will's mind.

Kyllard stood up and patted Jake's bare arm. "What do you see?"

Jake raised his arms to the air as if reaching for the invisible heavens hidden beyond the ceiling tiles. "I can see it," he whispered. "A thousand black flowers draped over a field of red grass. They're all for me. I can see it now. The light, it's so dark and welcoming." At his last word, his fingers collapsed into fists and he looked to the lone window in the stuffy room.

"Go to it." Kyllard opened the window and pointed to the moon.

Jake walked over to the open window and stuck his head into the air, the winds of another Halloween caressing his hair. One leg found its way through the window and he followed it with the other.

"Jake, no! Jake!" Will's words were muffled by the deafening static in his ears. Jake reached at the moon and in seconds he flung himself out of the window, body falling through the air like a lightweight mannequin. The static in Will's head subsided and all he could hear was the crunching of bone against concrete.

"Jake, no..." Will let his head drop down in sorrow.

Kyllard closed the window, last bits of wind blowing at the bottom of her silver hair. She stooped next to the long glass table and gently slid a finger alongside one of the bodies. Its mouth opened at her touch, thin tongue protruding from the dark hole. The being's brown and rotten teeth clamped together before its pupils danced underneath the absence of eyelids. Will felt bile rise at the top of his stomach and in a matter of moments it all flowed out of his mouth like a rogue river. It dribbled down his chest and collected on his lap.

Grin plastered on her now sweaty face, Kyllard took steps over to Will and placed her palms over his knees, just out of reach of the trickles of vomit. She said something that Will couldn't hear. She looked up at him and closed her eyes. "And now for you," she said, her hand finding its way to his heaving chest. The large man grabbed the base of Will's head and although he wanted to scream with his last bits of sanity, all he could do was let tears slip from his angry eyes.

Kyllard stood and both of her hands were now on his temples. She bowed her head, mumblings lost in carroty light. In a moment Will couldn't tell if his eyes were open or closed, elastic pinches of illumination flashing every few seconds. He heard the murmur of Sonia's voice and the sweet tinge of affection in his heart. His vision dissipated into a smoldering explosion of dizzying static and a quick rocket of bright light.

The Hum of Dead Stars

Moonlight dissipates into a cloud of clove smoke and my eyes adjust to the sight of an evaporating sea. Fingers tingle with the chill of another dying night as they grip the edge of a warm cigarette. Blood graces nicotine inside my poisoned heart and I wait for my skin to dry and crack under a thin layer of frost. One last drag and the remains of the cigarette fall off the balcony and dissolve somewhere between the mist and rocks below the house.

I walk into the bedroom and flip the switch next to the doorframe, killing lights showering a pretty face eager to drift back into slumber. She looks at me with a midnight gaze and flips golden bangs out of her face. "Come back to bed," she says.

Deep breaths and I nod, ignoring the flounce of cold covering my arms and legs. I slide under layers of wool blankets and she drapes a leg over mine, stubble colliding with goosebumps. It's not so easy to fall asleep anymore and even as I close my eyes and embrace the most beautiful woman left in the world, thoughts race to the tune of a thousand crying children. I force quiet into the most hollow portions of my brain and soon enough all I can hear are the momentary melodies of Chelsea's breaths. She's sleeping soundly and I wish I could do the same.

Wind whistles over an ocean that's seen better years and I can remember when Chelsea and I found this house, this sanctuary away from a world in which blue skies were replaced with endless nights. I force my eyelids shut and picture a summer lake glistening with sunlight. The future has become our present and what I miss the most isn't something that's within the reach of my bitter, tired fingers. Chelsea slides a hand up my abdomen, resting it on my chest. Purple-painted fingernails clash against pallid skin and a shiver of warmth glides throughout my blood.

An odd hum resonates constantly from the glitter of dead

stars. It leaves us forever haunted and more than afraid of our future. The jagged corners of another dream begin to pinch me as a symphony of dying waves crashes against the last bits of consciousness.

#

Eyes open and view an empty bed and I can hear Chelsea attempting to make breakfast in the kitchen. I yawn and catch the cold breeze from outside. Even with the few doors and windows of the house locked and barricaded, a thin rush of air always manages to seep in through unseen cracks. I swing my legs over the side of the bed and stare through the sliding doors of the bedroom.

Only a few months ago I got used to the company of the moon and there's a small part of me that feeds off its pallid glow. Sometimes I believe I don't miss the beaming rays of sunshine anymore.

Chelsea leans into the room, tight black t-shirt and the jeans she's worn everyday for the past two weeks. "Breakfast is on the table if you want anything," she says.

I shake my head and continue staring at the darkness of the fresh morning sky. "I'm not hungry."

She sighs and blows hair out of her face, pouting her lips. "You have to eat something. It's not going to make the situation any better if you turn against your own body. You need strength. Please, eat something, even if it's small."

"Okay." I stand up and take slow steps out of the bedroom and into the hallway. I can remember the framed pictures that once graced these walls, snapshots into the life of another family. After the earthquakes, we threw them in the trash, the ghosts of the house long forgotten. The four-second walk into the kitchen seems more like time in a coffin than anything else.

A few pieces of burnt toast adorn a plate of watery eggs. I sit and smile at Chelsea. She was never a good cook but I know deep down inside that she's been trying her best for the past few months. I shove a forkful of yellow into my mouth and chew. Chelsea sips juice out of a paper cup and asks me if I want any. I nod and she pours the last of a bottle of apple juice into her cup and slides it next to my plate. Before I notice, she's on my lap with her arms wrapped around my neck. Her tears feel like fire to my aching skin and I push her off of my torso.

She does this at least once a day and I can never blame her.

"I want to leave," she says in between deep breaths. "I don't want to be here anymore."

I force her arms to the side and gaze at a monolithic beauty, bleeding mascara over wet cheeks. "I don't want to be here either. But I'd rather be here spending my days with you than living death two hundred miles away. Home is gone."

My finger gently presses into the skin between her breasts, black fabric embracing me. "*This* is home now."

I can tell her smile is forced and she walks away. I finish my breakfast and place the soiled plate into the sink with the other dishes that neither of us has touched in days. Four or five months ago I would have yelled at Chelsea for leaving a mess in the kitchen but now I'm just grateful that we're both alive and well. Sometimes she cries for her mother and father, other days it's for her sister and the handful of friends that she kept close to her heart.

I resist the urge to walk into the bedroom to comfort her and instead sit quietly in the living room, watching the anathema of blue snow fall from the sky and coat the ruins of the world outside the house.

#

Chelsea and I were engaged before the events happened. We wanted a December wedding and the quiet voices in our hearts begged us to hold true to the date. The winter air held a crisp quality and I found a charcoal grey blazer buried deep in the bedroom closet. Chelsea's hair was parted in the middle, rising roots of black fighting an unnatural swoop of blonde. She braved the cold and wore a white tank top and green-tinted jeans.

She looked at me with carcinogen eyes and mascara the color of autumn chrysanthemums. She said three words and I kissed her, standing and swaying under dead tree limbs while descending ash danced in our hair and backs. For the first time in weeks a small sliver of pink light penetrated through the obsidian of the afternoon sky. We both smiled at this small marvel in our new world, hoping that it was a sign of hope, a sign of better days.

We sat against the lone rock in the remains of the garden and held each other until the snow started to drift against the comfort of our skin, bits of vanilla radiating with only a tinge of blue. I planted my elbow in the dark crevasse below the middle of the rock and Chelsea laid her head against my chest. She perked up at the sight of two rabbits hopping through the dead trees of the surrounding forest, signs of life after nature's funeral.

We remained perfectly still and watched the animals sniff around the ground, little paws barely imprinting the ash and snow. The smaller of the two had fur as white as virgin clouds and when it stood up I could see a small grey spot of fur the shape of a distorted heart on its chest. Its mate, black fur and eyes like two drops of gelled seawater, nudged its nose against our feet before running back into the remains of the forest.

The white rabbit followed suit and before long Chelsea and I had fallen asleep, each holding what was left of the world in our tired hearts.

#

Fuzzy vision and I hear Chelsea's voice. She's sitting next to me and I don't know how long I've been asleep in the living room. She stares straight ahead, as if entranced with the night sky. A splinter of moonlight splits her face diagonally. My hand finds its way to her lap and her fingers clasp onto mine, squeezing like she hasn't seen me in months. Her head tilts, lips gently pressing against mine. She tastes like fresh honeydew. We kiss for what feels like hours, our bodies warm with desire.

"We should make dinner," she says. "Are you hungry?"

I nod and place my lips on her head, the scent of old shampoo and daisies greeting my nostrils with eager flare. She stands up and smiles. "You stay here and relax. I'll start dinner."

I lift my legs to the other side of the couch and sigh. It's only when I catch the outline of movement against darkness that I run into the kitchen and grab Chelsea by the hand. She doesn't have to say a word, just runs to the bedroom and slams the door shut. We've been prepared for moments like these.

"What's out there?" Her question is muffled by two inches of pine. I can hear voices outside of the walls, bodies scratching the exterior of the house. I reach into the hallway closet and pull one of the three guns resting on the top shelf. The metal is cold and all I can picture is my father teaching me how to duck hunt when I was a boy.

I rest my head against the bedroom door. "Stay in there and don't move. I'm going to check out the front of the house."

Hands and forehead drip with sweat as I peek out the peephole of the front door. I'm greeted with nothing but the violent swaying of vapid tree limbs and an everlasting gaze into the black of night. Silence breaks and my eyes burn with a quick flash of white light, fingers losing their grip on the gun. I fall to the ground and hear the banging against the door, each vivid thump pounding my spine. I close my eyes and remember that if whoever's outside gets to me, they'll get to Chelsea.

An ounce of strength finds its way into my hands and I'm pushing the door, holding it closed. The locks jingle with fright.

I hear a long, winding screech and the force outside stops. I wait at least two full minutes with my heart beating as fast as a thousand horses before I stand up. My back slides against the door on the way up and part of me is surprised that it's still upright. Chelsea walks slowly into the hallway and hugs me. I hold onto to her with one arm and keep the gun raised in the air with the other. "What was it?"

I shake my head and turn an eye to the peephole. A swash of black on the other side, an array of golden lights flickering in the sky. I push Chelsea away from the door and motion for her to leave the hallway. She takes tiny steps backwards until I can only see white-painted fingernails gripping the edge of the living room entrance. The locks are eased open. I'm careful to keep my fingers wrapped around the handle of the gun. The knob turns and a frosty chill sneaks into the house, the scent of sugar and ice.

I stand on the doorway, gun poised and ready for an attack. I turn my back to the night and see two streaks painted on the front door, a silver vein entwined with a splash of red in the shape of a distorted 'V.'

The echoes of comfort fly away as I rush into the house and slam the door behind me.

#

The wool blanket wrapped around her, Chelsea sits silently on the couch in front of the living room window. "What if they come back? What if they break in here? What do we do?"

I've been holding the gun for almost two hours and I'm so tired that I fear my fingers are interwoven with the aged metal. The truth is that I don't know what to do if someone breaks into the house. "I don't know what to do," I say. "It was just a threat, Chelsea."

She throws the blanket to the floor, fuzzy red clashing with the vomit-colored carpet. She starts shouting and after a few minutes I can only close my eyes as a response. When she calms down, she picks up the blanket and tosses it on the couch. She's wearing tight grey sweatpants that make her legs look like knives. Before she can leave the room I pull her into me so close that she's lifted off the ground. One deep kiss and her hands are tugging at the back of my head, slender fingers pulling brown hair.

"I'm not going to let anything happen to you," I say. "I love you. I would have rather died four months ago than know there'd be a day I'd have to live without you."

The subtle twinkle in the cavernous green of her eyes is all I need right now. She holds my hand, palms sticking together with a millimeter of sweat. Chelsea's head eases into my chest and her eyelids open and close to the rhythm of my breaths.

"Whoever they are," I say, "will never get past me. Nothing will happen to you, I promise."

She presses her lips against my cheek and leaves the room. "You can't sit there all night. You need some sleep."

"I know. I'm going to sit up for a little while."

Her footsteps into the kitchen are soft murmurs against the pink lightning storm raging outside. Cherry slices of light break through the darkness, each one shining long enough to see the outlines of every remaining star adorning the night sky. If I close my eyes the peculiar drone beyond the living room window will fill my head. Each note is like code, informing who's left in the world that the earth is evolving into something different. I can only imagine what lies beyond the balcony. And I can only imagine who left their markings on our front door. We haven't seen signs of life since the trek into the mountains nearly four months ago.

I sit up and walk through the kitchen. I haven't eaten all day and have no desire to do so now. Chelsea and I are sick of eating canned food three times a day but we both know that luck was on our side when we found a stockpile of food and bottled water in the cabinets and cupboard.

A supple ginger glow spills out of the bedroom. It makes my shadow look like a hunchback, my head and arms bent forward. My fingers slide against the wall, squishy steps on the bedroom carpet as I view the striking silhouette of Chelsea's body. She squeaks out a small "hello" with a seductive smile. She was blessed with the curves of a tattooed angel and a voice that could make a man cry.

"Come to bed," she says.

Pretty soon my clothes are on the floor and I forget that the world has ended.

#

I wake up alone in bed, the leftover scent of sex and lavender floating above my bare body. Chelsea was never one for sleeping in. When we first lived together, she'd wake up much earlier than me and go out for a run or make breakfast. I guess she's still in the habit even though night has eroded most of the light of every cold morning.

I swing my legs over the side of the bed and put on jeans and a t-shirt. My hoodie slouches over my shoulder as I head into the kitchen and see Chelsea sitting silently at the kitchen table, reading a newspaper. She looks up and a tiny smile curls at the bottom of her face, a sliver of delight amidst light freckles. Her head bows back to the newspaper and after a minute I realize that I haven't watched the news on television or read a magazine or newspaper since the sun's rays first carved through comet dust.

Chelsea flips a page and lifts her head to me, giving me a quick kiss on the cheek. I run fingers alongside parts of her matted curls, crunching the hardened hair from day-old hairspray. She looks as beautiful as she did the night before.

I lean in and see that she's reading *The Great Falls Tribune* from March 6, 2015. She can see the inquisitive look on my face, probably the way my eyebrows flare against the pale skin of my forehead. "I haven't read anything since we got here," she says. "I just want to feel like the world is alive and breathing again." She raises the newspaper, her eyes scanning words that mean nothing now.

I nod and sit next to her, easing into the pine chair and taking a deep breath. My body wants breakfast but my mind needs fresh air. "I'm going to take a quick walk outside. Do you want to come?"

"Do you think it's safe?" She frowns.

"I think we'll be okay."

She folds the newspaper and zips up her sweatshirt. I can tell she's not wearing a bra; nipples poke through two thin layers of cloth. She reaches out for my hand and I hold onto it as we walk out of the kitchen and through the front door. The markings on the door behind us, neither of us mention their creation or what they mean. We follow the small trail around the house leading up to the edge of the property, the balcony just above us. Only a small amount of light provides guidance to the end of the trail. We look over the side, cerulean mist circling above the rocks, the last breaths of a dissolving stream. Chelsea squeezes my arm, her slender fingers tightening around muscle and fabric. "We'll go inside in a few minutes," I tell her.

I can read fear in the words lost somewhere between her eyes, unease flowing in her weary blood. A sniff of air and I know that the world doesn't smell the same without leaves and trees and animals. I used to work in the city and every day cursed the bustle of metro life. As I take a few steps to the edge of the rocks, I realize that I'd give my own soul to be lying in the apartment bed with Chelsea, a concert of blaring traffic on the streets outside.

The rocks sturdy beneath my boots, I edge further until a blanket of mist wraps around my legs. Chelsea stays behind, standing with her arms crossed, eyes now two slits of green.

When we first found the house the sounds of crashing waves below us put our minds at ease, as if our destructive present was offset by an inkling of normality. We noticed the waters of the rivers start to evaporate only a month ago. Everyday the fog rising from the base of the mountain grows thicker and it's only a matter of time before yet another aspect of our world fades into nothing.

It's amazing to think that we haven't seen the sun in months yet the surface the earth hasn't frozen over. I know it's somewhere behind the blanket of obsidian, afraid to shower its old world with healthy streams of light.

Chelsea calls out to me, the trickling of her squeaky voice reaching me as I find my last step on the rocks. A gigantic breath of misty air and my lungs soothe with a comfortable taste. It's all I needed this morning. I walk back to the trail and Chelsea pulls my hand until we're pacing on the dirt. "I don't like it out here," she says.

"Neither do I."

Before we reach the house, I look back to the lifeless woods surrounding the trail. A path of fire shoots across the horizon like a scarlet laser, piercing a constellation of stars. Chelsea puts a hand over her mouth and looks at me. We stand in awe for a few minutes, the next comet shooting across a coverlet of cobalt green, its tail withering into tiny sparks and silent explosions. I hold Chelsea's hand in mine, squeezing her fingers with each flare. The only sounds I can hear are the purrs of the remaining stars and our disparate breaths.

We walk into the house and close the front door behind us, the dead of silence greeting us with open arms. Chelsea removes her sweatshirt and tosses it to the floor. I stand behind her and rub her arms, trying to warm her skin with just my fingertips. My lips find the back of her neck, giving her a few quick kisses before she pulls away. She turns around and smiles, returning the kisses with her own.

"I love you," she says. "Every day I wake up and think I'm dreaming. I think I'm in a recurring nightmare."

"Me too."

"What are we going to do?"

"I don't know, Chelsea. All I'm thinking about is staying alive."

She sighs and shoves her hands into her front jean pockets. "I have a horrible feeling that this isn't the right place for us to be."

I close my eyes, trying to funnel the warmth from my heart into the rest of my body. "We should be dead right now. We're lucky that we're here. We're lucky that we're both breathing, sleeping, eating and spending time together."

"I know. I'll just never get used to this place."

A shiver slithers up my legs and creeps into my spine. Cold dominates the room, a swoop of electric frost sticking to the windows. I look outside and the lightshow has ended, the night skies just an infinite coverlet of black.

#

Los Angeles was buried under a mile-high wave of water. Planes fell from the sky like birds hunted on a crisp autumn day. We were lucky enough to be on the road after visiting Chelsea's parents in Salt Lake City. We kept driving north until we couldn't hear the screams anymore, the chilling voices of a dying race. I can't remember the last time we saw the sun, the last time I sat outside with a smile.

#

The radio stopped broadcasting noise three weeks ago. Until then, I'd spend every morning scrolling through the frequencies, eager to hear even the most subtle of human voices. The FM stations were mostly all static, a few transmitting barebones silence. Chelsea would sit next to me, biting her fingernails and hoping to hear any signs of life beyond our own private world.

What startled us even more than the lack of existence was on the AM frequencies: each station played the same odd hum that fell from the stars. Its drone almost hypnotic, we sat close to each other as I fumbled through each frequency, the only sounds sneaking from the speakers making our skin crawl with terrible delight. I didn't want to know what the sounds meant, didn't want to decode the throbbing waves recoiling on each side of my brain.

I switched the dial back to FM and felt an abnormal comfort with the resonance of static.

I haven't looked at the radio since. I sit with a plastic cup filled with vodka and warm cranberry juice, staring at the dusty shelves around the basement, each adorned with cans and cans of vegetables, fruit and beans. I know that at some point down the road we're going to run out of food, but my mind hasn't thought that far ahead into our future. I don't want to know what's going to happen the day we need to leave the house to find food and water.

Chelsea jogs down the stairs, her boots clicking against aged wood. "Are you okay?"

"Yeah, I'm fine. Just wanted to sit somewhere for a bit where there were no windows."

"Dinner's ready. Why don't you come upstairs and eat with me?"

I force a smile and finish my drink, crumbling the paper cup and tossing it to the floor. It lands next to a lawnmower covered with grime. I follow Chelsea up the steps, closing the basement door behind me and locking it.

We eat a mix of baked beans and creamed corn, each of us filling our glasses with one of the many bottles of wine that were hidden away in the kitchen cabinets. Chelsea's cheeks fill with red spots and I know that she was drinking while she cooked dinner. Her eyes are watery, broken emeralds shimmering with a thin layer of tears. I don't ask if she's okay. I finish my plate and split it in half, paper snapping us out of our quiet trances.

Chelsea still at the table, I leave and open another bottle of wine. A big gulp flowing down my throat, I head into the living room, plopping down on the couch like I've worked a twelve-hour day. Long sips and long gazes before I'm lost somewhere in the fuzzy confines of slumber.

#

Chelsea's scream floats from the corners of a dream world, clouds hiding urgency. My eyes open to the reality of her desperate pleas and before I realize it I'm on my feet and running into the kitchen. Chilly air flows freely from the broken kitchen window, angora curtains shifting from side to side in a violent motion.

Chelsea is huddled in the corner, hair draped over her face like she's hiding from the outside world. I grab her by the arm and pull until she's running behind me. We run into the bedroom and slam the door. "Stay in here. I'm going back out there."

I pull the closet door open and snatch the gun on the shelf, clicking the safety off and glaring at Chelsea before leaving her. She reaches for the shotgun under the bed and crawls into the corner of the room. It all happens in slow motion. I ease my steps from the hallway into the kitchen, careful to not let my boots squeak against the wooden floor.

The gun aimed in front of me, I swing into the kitchen and see a black figure hop from behind the table and into the living room. My breaths panicked and heavy, I follow it until the shadow disappears. All I can see is a figure draped in black, not an inch of skin peeking from its clothing. A quick burst of red and I'm on the floor, pain wriggling the nerves in my face, gun thrown too many feet away from me. Through hazy vision, its legs scuttle past me and I hear the breaking of glass.

I roll over and onto my feet and hurry into the kitchen, leaving the gun on the carpeted floor behind me. Nothing but the hurried stream of air sliding against my face, I lean over the sink and look out the broken window, careful not to scrape my chest on the battered glass. The night whistles with uncertain glee, the intruder long gone by now. The blood dripping from my nose leaks into my mouth and it tastes like tinfoil.

I knock twice on the bedroom door, Chelsea barely opening it. I see a bit of dirty blonde hair, fingernails digging into the door. "Stay in here," I say. "I need to board up the kitchen window." I can't hear what she says before I turn the knob to me and pull with all of my force.

Two markings are engraved into the kitchen table. A silver streak crosses a longer stripe of red, making an upside-down 'V.' I shudder and force myself to walk away.

The basement is darker than the skies outside. I stumble down the stairs, nearly tripping over my own feet. Fumbling through the trash on the floor next to the generator, I find a piece of wood much larger than the size of the window. I don't have time to keep searching so I throw it by the bottom of the stairs and find the toolbox we keep on top of the refrigerator. Another crash upstairs, not nearly as loud as the one before. A gunshot rings and blows past the silence of the basement. I let out a muffled scream, the moan of a frightened child.

I reach the top of the basement stairs and see my love covered in blood, crimson spots dancing on her white t-shirt. Smoke glides from the hot barrel and disappears into the ceiling. Chelsea falls to the floor, dropping the shotgun. The sound of her crying is the loudest noise I've ever heard in my life.

The body is crumpled against one of the kitchen chairs, its legs curled. I can see that it's an older man with hair the color of polished brass. His eyes are open and his chest is absent of breaths. Black and torn fabric reveals multiple patches of freshly penetrated skin.

"He pushed open the bedroom door," Chelsea says. "I shot him, Konrad. I had to shoot him."

I reach for her hand and she grips it harder than she ever has before. Holding on to her, I reach for the man's wrist. His heart has stopped beating and his cold, dead body left this world with a filthy stare at my wife.

"Go get a towel and clean off. **Now.**"

She runs to the bathroom. I push the man's eyelids down, flaps of skin covering the coldest stare to grace this lonely house. His arms are as heavy as tree trunks and it's tough to pull him out of the kitchen. I let the body fall down the basement stairs, watching the skull smack the concrete wall, bits of blood smearing the marine blue stone. I trot along the steps, finding the toolbox and sheet of wood.

Running back upstairs, I drop it on the kitchen floor and slam the basement door behind me. Chelsea is in the bathroom, wearing a lacy pink bra. She sits against the sink, head down and solemn. Her soiled t-shirt is crumpled in the trash barrel amidst a mess of wet paper towels. I put my arms around her and press my lips against her forehead. Her sweat is sweet, like sugar water.

It only takes me five minutes to board up the window. When I'm done, I take a swig of wine and drink until it spills out of my mouth and drips on my shirt and the floor. It takes me a few moments to collect myself and realize what happened over the last ten minutes. I ease into one of the kitchen's chairs and finish the bottle of wine before letting my mind calm to the tune of the nighttime's ambient melody.

#

Chelsea stands next to the living room window, the hands of a woman gracing the shotgun like it was a sleeping child. She watches the trees sway back and forth, waiting for any sign of movement in the darkness surrounding the house. I drift in and out of consciousness, eyes following Chelsea in the silent filmstrip of my mind. Before long, I sit up and she's gone, leaving me with a square portrait of absolute black. The wine leaves pulses of tenderness beating just behind my eyes, the remains of a violent evening.

I slip out of the living room, ignoring patterns of candlelight dancing against the hallway floor. Footsteps are gentle and slide against the linoleum floor in a seamless motion. I stand before the basement door and take a deep breath before opening it. The steps come slowly, my boots lending weight until the wood creaks with an awkward moan.

The intruder's body is slouched at the bottom of the stairs. His eyelids are still closed, the fury once raging in his arms and legs now dormant in insipid skin. I poke his chest with a bitter finger and wince, part of me expecting that the corpse will return to full life. His pants are thick and soiled and smell like fresh dirt. I search his two pockets and find nothing. The head tilts to the side when I remove my hand. I jump back in reaction, each thud of my heart nearly popping through my ribcage. I stand up and notice the black marks on the left side of his neck. Leaning down, I see the amateur tattoo scrawled into the skin. It's a sideways V and at this very moment all I can picture is Chelsea crying in her room, clutching the eggshell white blankets while trails of veins fill with anxious blood.

I kick the body once, twice. It doesn't move. Curses fill the room and my eyes start to water. I wipe away the discharge, running up the basement stairs and letting the cool indoor air graze past my cheeks as it shoves the door shut behind me. Ovals of light my guide, I follow them until I reach the bedroom door. Chelsea sleeps on the very edge of the bed, like a frightened dog. I'm careful not to startle her as I kick off my boots and fall into the mess of pillows and blankets.

The world rages on outside of our house and all I can do is let the tears flow as I nestle my head next to the golden curls of my wife's hair.

#

Two days have passed and neither of us has ventured outside. It's only now that I've learned to accept the radiance of noise crinkling in the night sky, its mellow drone sliding into my ears in hypnotic fashion. Chelsea lies naked under the sheet and says that she can't hear it anymore.

"How?"

"All I can hear is the shotgun blast," she says. "The weight of his body slamming against the kitchen chairs."

I nod and understand that to kill someone is to accept seeing the person's face every time you close your eyes. Chelsea turns to me with the look of desperation, eyes eager to confess their sins with only a single glance. The bed sheets barely cover her body up to her chest.

"This isn't going to last forever," she says.

I won't answer her. Instead, I stare at the collection of stains on the bedroom ceiling, follow the collection with my hand as more words creep out of her mouth. I say nothing and get out of bed, waiting a moment before putting on my jeans and t-shirt.

"Please listen to me," Chelsea says. "We have to think about leaving. I don't want to die."

Head down, I let my toes curl against the carpet. It takes all of my willpower to stay silent, but only a phrase escapes my lips. "We're not going anywhere."

I blow out the candle on the dresser and find my boots, ignoring the waves of sound pounding on my skull. Chelsea closes the door after I leave. I sit at the kitchen table, my fingernails trying to pick off the dry chips of black and red paint. I don't know the interpretation of the symbol but every time I see it I know that Chelsea's right. It's not safe here anymore but leaving the mountains will only guarantee that both of our lives will end under harsh circumstances.

It's only a matter of time before whoever's outside will break in again.

It's only a matter of time before death comes knocking again.

I find another bottle of wine buried behind rows of canned vegetables. Jade glass covers blood red liquid and before I pop open the cork, Chelsea grabs the bottle from me and smashes it to the ground. Tiny shards split and waltz into the air, drops of merlot splashing against banana-colored linoleum. She's taking deep breaths, small breasts sulking under a thin layer of purple fabric. She shakes her head, disappointment rising from white knuckles.

She clenches her teeth and leaves the kitchen. For a moment her aura floats behind her, a simple pattern of translucent lace crawling into the air. I rub my eyes, letting leftover sleep dig into my retinas. "Chelsea…"

She doesn't answer and within a matter of seconds I hear the bedroom door crash with unbridled might. I sigh and start to clean up the mess on the kitchen floor. Paper towels soak up the dirty residue of wine, leaving a trail of orange spots on the kitchen floor. I'm on my knees, dropping the towels into one of the last plastic trash bags we have left when Chelsea walks back into the kitchen, pallid skin drained of every drop of emotion.

Her lips curl and I ask what's wrong. She just turns her head back to the bedroom, a simple motion that beckons me to follow her. I take her hand and she leads me through darkness and into the bedroom where our bodies are lit by an array of lights. I step away from Chelsea and edge closer to the bedroom window, my hand shoving away the few inches covered by curtains. The moon hovers amongst the night sky, a bright eye looking down upon a scarred planet. In a matter of moments, the moon's center pops in a vivid flash. It looks like a giant orange rose set to fire, purple streaks entwined with space glitter and tinges of silver.

Chelsea presses her body against mine but I barely notice. "Oh my God," she says. She squeezes the loose ends of my t-shirt, tugging on the cloth like a child clutching its father. We stand for what feels like hours, watching the celestial destruction unfold in the sky. Gold light spills into the room and for a moment I look away, my vision locked on Chelsea's tranquil face. The green in her eyes mixes with shimmering moonlight, like emeralds floating in a sea of melting bronze.

I pull Chelsea to the bed, my hands on her hips. Breaths of sorrow take flight from my lips as flickers of dust begin to drop from the remaining stars. Chelsea lies next to me and a frightening calm creeps into my chest, every heartbeat forcing hair to stand on end. Her body nuzzled against me, we eventually drift into a dreamless slumber, an outline of igniting flowers burnt to the backdrop of our eyelids.

#

I sit up in bed, alone and tired. The blankets are crumpled at the edge of the bed. I reach over to the opposite side of the bed, expecting my hand to be greeted with the warmth of Chelsea's skin. Fingers find nothing but cool sheets and my own shadow. My stomach growls, feeding off of the remains of slumber. I force myself out of bed and close the curtains.

I stumble out of the bedroom and walk into the kitchen. The large board surprises me and after a few seconds I remember what happened a couple nights ago. Chelsea isn't in the kitchen or in the living room. After checking the bathroom, a chilly wind lurches into my bones. The front door is wide open, the air barely able to rustle its sturdy frame. In a moment of panic, I grab the gun from our bedroom and run outside, my boots scraping against the dirt trail. The moon is nowhere to be found, replaced by a swash of stars the color of morning bruises. I see her hair tossed by a winter wind, whorls of curly locks spattered in multiple directions. The gun stuck inside the back of my jeans, I jog to Chelsea and stop just a few feet away from her.

She stands with her arms covering her stomach. I take a step next to her and whisper into her ear. "Chelsea, honey, are you okay?"

She closes her eyes in response, violet eyeliner gleaming with spatters of glitter. She takes a deep breath and takes a step forward, closer to the edge of rocks. Ashen swirls of mist circle around us and when I try to slide a hand into her crossed arms she pushes me away. "We can't live like this any longer. It's not worth it."

"Chelsea, please. Come back inside the house and we'll talk."

She shakes her head, moving her arms to the side and opening her eyes. "No, I don't want to go back in there. I'm not going to waste away in there."

Chelsea steps further, her pink sneakers now hugging the slab of grey rocks. Another few inches and she could fall. She starts to speak again but my arms are already around her waist, lifting her into the air. She kicks away the mist rising from the decaying mountain stream, screaming at the top of her lungs. The noise rattles the bones in my face. She attempts to fight her way out of my grip the entire walk back to the house. I set her down at the set of four concrete stairs at the bottom of the front door.

"Calm down, please."

She lets her head fall and starts to cry, thick tears falling from her face and smacking the stone beneath our feet. I kneel in front of her, placing my hands on the sides of her head, soft rumples of hair touching my skin.

"What's wrong?"

Chelsea sniffles and looks at me, smudges of mulberry wet with salt and sorrow. Her frown is almost icy and I have to look away. She holds onto my hand and I can barely hear what she says under the whine of my own thoughts.

"I'm pregnant."

Blood in my heart quickens and in seconds Chelsea's eyes glow with the reflection of scattered fireflies.

#

Chelsea sleeps with her head on my chest. I can remember the first night we slept together. She was twenty-three years old and it took every ounce of resistance to keep myself from proposing after only a week of dating. Only a couple of years later, we're sitting alive after the earth's funeral with a baby baking in her womb. She said that it wouldn't be fair to raise a child in this new world. Wouldn't be fair to bring life into a world that was so filled with death.

She wanted to end her own life to avoid creating a new one. She said I was the reason she didn't jump into the remains of the river. I was the reason why she wanted to continue to live.

I ease myself out of her grasp and head into the kitchen, careful not to wake her. The wine calls out to me but even in celebration I know that the sweet taste of alcohol wouldn't be respectful. I pour a small glass of water and sit at the kitchen table, wondering if the ideas running through my head were the same ones my own father experienced so many years ago.

The liquid soothes my throat. I sit for a few minutes more, trying to ignore the remains of the intruder's etching scrawled into the surface of the kitchen table. My palm slides over the markings and a slight chill runs up my arm and into the muscles. I finish the water and drop the glass into the sink next to a growing pile of filthy china.

"Hey baby," Chelsea says.

I'm alarmed at the tinny peep in her voice and turn around with a fist. "Sorry, I didn't think you were awake."

She smiles and sits at the table, rolling the sleeves of her sweater past her wrists to the middle of her hand. "It's okay.

We've been on edge since we found this place."

I sit next to her and she immediately curls her fingers over my hand. Her cheeks are as red as poinsettias. "We're having a baby," she says with a grin. "**A baby.**"

"I know." My voice twinkles with the type of delight that neither of us have experienced before.

I'm just about ready to ask Chelsea what she wants for dinner when I hear a screeching bang in the living room. We both stand up, the light of terror sprinkled in our eyes. "Not again," I say. I rush to the bedroom, Chelsea behind me, and grab the shotgun. It hasn't been touched since she shot the intruder just days ago. It feels powerful in my arms, almost a living, breathing entity soaking up the weight of my arms.

"Stay here, I'll be right back."

Chelsea closes and locks the door behind me. Long strides to the living room turns into a full run, another snapping crunch striking the walls. The front door is shoved off its hinges before I'm there, bolts and screws tossed into the night air. Three figures stand before me, each dressed in black. I raise the shotgun but before I can pull the trigger I'm brought to the ground by someone behind me. His hands knock the shotgun across the living room floor and in only a second I feel the clout of a wooden plank against my face.

"Get the girl," one of them says.

Springs of pain rush into my eyes, my cheekbones. My breaths are panicked and all I can see are flickering spots of white. The man keeps his arms on mine, movement stifled by his grimy body. The three other shapes walk past me and into the kitchen. I can barely see them now, only wads of black against the blood dripping into my eyes. Chelsea's apocalyptic scream pierces the air and everything is starting to fade away.

The last thing that comes across my vision is my wife's body dragged across the carpeted floor, her golden hair now just a distant memory.

#

Jarring flashes of pewter poke me out of sleep. I turn over to see the shotgun leaning against the loveseat in the corner of the living room. My tongue finds a small hard object in my mouth. I spit it out and see it's one of a few teeth that are missing from my jaw.

Moonlight drips into the room through the broken living room window and I say one name before shouting as loud as I've ever had before. *Chelsea.*

I frantically run to each part of the house, the basement. She's not here and after a few seconds I remember the figures dragging her across the floor. My wife, my love. Gone.

My father used to say that men's tears were a different color than women's. I look in the bathroom mirror and see a torrent of salty water shooting from my eyes, each arc of every tear burning the bruises and cuts in my battered face. They look darker, as if my glands started producing secretion as black as motor oil. I can't feel my heart beating and I could die right here in the bathroom, clutching my heart while calling out the names of everyone I've ever known.

There's only one name I need to hear and I don't have the strength to speak it out loud again.

I leave the bathroom and stagger into the kitchen, try to picture Chelsea cooking at the stove, a tight white t-shirt cut just below the belly button. My eyes closed, I walk into the living room and feel the chill of a winter breeze. The front door lies on the floor, digging into the carpet. The outside air is cold and unforgiving and when I see their symbol splattered against the front entrance's landing I kneel to the ground. They took my wife but I wish they had taken me instead. My child could be breathing, unknowing of the world outside his mother's skin.

I take a few steps along the sandy trail, kicking dirt into the air. The ethereal hum of the stars is gone, replaced by lifeless silence. I walk around the house twice before going back inside, stepping on the front door as I enter. I expect to see Chelsea leaning into the living room, swinging by one arm gracing the edge of the entryway.

I'm greeted by nothing except a blood-stained carpet and regret.

A familiar shine hops across the kitchen walls and I remember the nights when Chelsea would read by candlelight, her legs crossed and head perched by a fist. Her hair would hang over her eyes and I would always ask how she could see in between the long, frosty curls.

The bedroom smells like burnt cinnamon. I notice the tip of something small and brown placed in the center of the bed. It's a bag made of burlap, tied with dirty brown string. It feels like two squishy marbles and I drop it to the floor, not wanting to open it. Deep breaths eclipse a wearied heart and I force myself to pick it up and open it.

The string comes undone with a simple twitch and the bag falls apart in my hands, each corner easing open. What I hold is something that I've stared at for too many months. What I hold is the beautiful siren that lured me to my wife in the very beginning. What I hold convinces me that she's far away and dead.

I bring my hand to my face and Chelsea's eyes glare back at me, devoid of life and filled with the lost echoes of hope. Red strands of muscle squiggle out of the bloody sheath and I drop them to the ground, hoping that my skull will collapse and fill my brain with the music of the departed.

I just held my wife's eyes in my hands and now I know that I'll never see her again. Her life was wasted in this new world.

Bed sheets holding my body, I slide into the pillows and try to remember Chelsea's voice. I can only hear it if I close my eyes. Lips kiss the edge of the pillow, my drool spilling onto the soft fabric of my wife's pillow. It still smells like her. With a last ounce of vigor, my legs find the bedroom floor and I blow out the candle, the syrupy aroma of butterflies arousing the air around me. Through the darkness, I make my way into the closet, throwing her jeans and old blouses aside. The handgun is cold to the touch. I wrap my fingers around the handle and shut the bedroom door, forever leaving the scent of Chelsea behind me.

#

The stars mock me as I walk along the trail at the front of the house. I look to the sky with eyes of rage, blaming them for the demise of life and love. The only sound penetrating the night air is the scraping of my boots against dirt and rock.

The gun is jammed in the back of my jeans. I wait until I reach the back of the house to pull it out, holding it high in front of me, both hands aiming it towards the moon. I stand before the rock where Chelsea and I confirmed our love for each other, the exact spot where we were married. I toss the gun to the ground and it lands in a bed of lifeless flowers, slate gray metal slamming against the only withered petals that didn't blow away in the wind.

I kneel into the rock, my face pressed against the lone crevasse in the middle of the weathered stone. A steady flow of tears falls and coats the rock.

I cry for my mother and father, my little brother who was in college when it all went to hell. My grandparents were deep beneath the ground and were spared the wrath of destruction. I think of Chelsea and the tears stop. I remember the promise I made to her and realize that I broke it into a million little pieces. Wiping my face, I reach over and pick up the gun, gaze at it for a minute. I never owned a weapon until we found this house.

Wind whips at my back, my thin jacket flapping and smacking against the skin. I peel it off and throw it to the side, watch it drift against the edge of rocks and fall over, the outline of my soul descending with it as it disappears into whatever is left of the river below the mountains.

I kick off my sneakers, shake the dirt and sand out of the soles before I throw them over the side of the mountain. The black rubber blends with the darkness and soon they're out of sight. Sitting on the rock, my toes push away a pile of dead leaves. They crumble into a pile of dark green dust and blow away.

My legs hanging over the front of the rock and my back to the open air, I shove the gun in my mouth, teeth clamping down on the barrel. My tongue licks the bottom of the metal, a strange flavor that reminds me of overcooked coffee. Bits of rain descend from whatever clouds lurk behind a wall of black static. They hit my swollen face and the wetness comforts the cuts and bruises.

I hum a song to say goodbye, the last tune of my life will be built on my own accord. Chelsea's voice joins me and my finger rests against the trigger. I can feel the rising mist sneak up my t-shirt, colliding with sweat and sticking to my back.

Eyes open to take a final view of the world and I can see Chelsea walk along the trail. She's wearing all white, a skirt ending just above the knee. Her silhouette disappears as slivers of lightning begin to pierce the horizon. I'm left with just my shadow.

I scoot over closer to the edge of the rock, hoping that when the bullet shatters the back of my skull, gray matter and bits of bloodied bone will tumble down the mountain and hit the ground before my body does.

I'm ready, Chelsea.

Just when I'm about to end it a fluffy shape of white enters my vision. It comes closer, stopping at the edge of the woods before I can see what it is. The rabbit, fur as virginal as a summer morning, grey blotch shaped like a heart on its chest. It scoots over to me, only an inch away from my toes. It sniffs the bottom of my foot and for a moment I swear its tiny eyes glance up at me.

I look up to the sky, say her name only once. Wherever she is,

I know she's smiling. I know she's holding our child, giving it a kiss on the forehead for me.

Lips grow cool from the barrel of the gun and I pull it out of my mouth, gently rest it on my lap. The rabbit scampers away, hops into the woods and disappears. A smile finds its way across my face.

Standing up, I turn to the edge of the mountain. Fog makes way for the gun as I toss it as far as I can, watching the little black dot fade into a cloud of incandescence. I imagine the sun setting for Chelsea, for me, a veil of grey embracing the remains of a world that took everything away.

This is only the beginning.

Coralee

The moon explodes into a thousand fiery fragments of glitter and dust. Fourteen seconds, a breath and the needle prick squeezes a glowing trail of euphoric lava into my bloodstream. I tilt my head back, ignore the wails of the many ghosts swimming beneath my skull. Time becomes incidental and every second I'm awake is another lost moment that will be forgotten. The needle falls to the carpeted motel floor and wraps itself in the footsteps of the past lives of this room, this cocoon.

I can't tell if I'm sitting, standing or floating. Whispers slither across the walls like angry wraiths. The curtains sway from side to side as if pushed and pulled by unseen forces. The figures on the television screen are hollow, eyes like black hollow sockets. The marching band in my head pounds another tune and their tiny little footsteps are an ethereal symphony. I never knew that I've waited weeks for this day to come and the physical portions of my body are the only ones ready for it all to come down.

Down, I peer, watching a pack of blue ants step across the carpet with a focused purpose, their antennae like radiant glowsticks. It takes nearly a full minute to stand up and when I do the television screen shifts to an array of static and gray noise. The motel's ancient pipes wheeze with age and for a moment I pretend that I'm back at home, back with her. I wonder if she's flying above the city, searching for the next great soul to fix.

My Coralee, the one who came, the one who went. The one who left me here.

It hasn't been long since she's been gone and already I can feel the obsidian rats eating at the edge of my heart. It's only a matter of time before they penetrate the fleshy fibers around it and claw their way inside.

Her touch was enough to dull the pain, but yet not enough to keep me from this poison now careening through my veins.

Coralee, where are you?

And to think, she came along at just the right moment in my life, as if a divine architect swooped our timelines over one another just to see the graceful union of destruction and grace. I can remember the minute, the second, as if it were only this afternoon.

The white tinges of pain pinch at my chest. Only a few hours, maybe. And to think it didn't have to end like this.

#

He had the look of a fallen soldier, bright blue eyes under a sheen of distress. He flipped the first page over the back of the clipboard and shook his head once, twice. Pen firmly gripped in his right hand, he scribbled for a few seconds before tossing the clipboard onto the desk behind him.

"Not much difference from last week," Dr. O'Connell said. "Trent, I'm sorry. "

I nodded. That's all I ever did here, listening to him talk about how there was never a change in my condition. We went through this every week. He probably knew more about me than my parents.

"I know, doc," I said. "You don't have to say anything else."

Dr. O'Connell smiled and pointed to the scars on my arm. The left one, that is, because, when I was younger, I refused to use the other. I figured that I'd at least need one of them if the other failed me after all the shit I'd injected into it over the years.

"I wish there was something else I could do. How long have you been on the list now?"

I forced a smile. "Too long."

Dr. O'Connell shook his head. It was almost funny to think that he was no more than a year or two older than me, yet we were standing on two completely opposite sides of life. He put a hand on my shoulder, as he always did right after my dialysis session, and squeezed the fabric of my shirt. "Don't give up, Trent. Hang in there. See you in, what, two days?"

I buttoned up the top few buttons of my dress shirt. "You know it, Doc."

Dr. O'Connell left the room and white streams of sunlight followed closely behind. I walked past the emergency room front desk, threw a smile at the nurse tapping away at a bulky computer, and made my way into an elevator to the cafeteria on the first floor. When I first started coming here, I couldn't wait to leave, to get away from the smell of faux orange disinfectant and plastic. I'd often fall asleep in the chair, an attempt to force my mind to dream about anything, everything. But now, I figure I owe this place. They've kept me alive for nearly three years after I ravaged my body and mind, so now I stop by the cafeteria for a coffee before getting on with the day.

I ordered a coffee, dumped three packets of sugar into the cup, and found a seat at the very corner of the cafeteria. It was moments like these that a man who had this affliction would stop to collect himself, maybe figure out a better path for the future that didn't involve a casket. Trent Howarth wasn't like that and he could swear that his stubbornness eclipsed that of even his drunken, absentee father.

A sip of the black brew warmed my throat and I closed my eyes, and repeated the process until at least ten minutes had passed. It was right here that I first saw her, charcoal hoodie and piercing emerald eyes that could start a war. She had been staring out one of the many cafeteria windows, pale fingers wrapped around a coffee cup. She didn't notice me until I walked past a few minutes later, and offered a small grin before continuing her focus on the autumn foliage of another Boston afternoon.

In the days since she left, I replayed that one visual, that one smile, in the celluloid behind my brain at least a thousand times.

After depositing my cup in the receptacle near the cafeteria entrance, I left the hospital behind me like so many times before.

#

The September sun was beginning its descent into the lavender sky beyond Boston Common's army of dying trees. A breeze crept from the west and if it wasn't for the crisp snap of its cool embrace, I would have fallen into a calm slumber at the edge of the park. I fished around my front jeans pocket and grabbed a small white pill. The '512' imprint was often a sign of comfort, of familiarity. I popped it onto the back of my throat and sent it on its way. Within minutes, streaks of sunlight bled from the sky like melting vanilla frost. Passersby were momentary cartoon figures, each one walking past in slow motion with a trail of comet dust not far behind.

The sky went dark for only a moment, my eyes adjusting to the embrace of the painkiller. I nearly let the black hole pull me away, but she was there, kneeling in front of me, last bits of sunlight forming a cracked halo above her head.

"Wake up," she said. "Come on, wake up."

I opened my mouth, tried to find my words.

Her cheeks crumped into pale dimples. "I saw you at the hospital a few hours ago. Recognized you just as I was about to head down into the train station at the edge of the Common."

"Ah," was all I could get out before she reached for my hand. The touch was almost like an anesthetic, my vision becoming clearer, my body back to an undamaged state.

"You need a coffee." She pulled me towards the eastern edge of the Common, black, chipped fingernails intertwined with my bruised and battered hand. Upon our touch, I could see the memories of my childhood, the times before my life went to shit.

"Here," she said. "I go to this place everyday."

She turned to me and smiled. It was as if I had known her all of my life.

#

Her name was Coralee and she said she was from New York City. I sipped my coffee tenderly, smiled when I could. The dim light of the coffeehouse allowed the arctic blue of her eyes to sparkle like the tips of broken icebergs.

"That wasn't the first time I saw you at Mass General, was it?"

I shook my head. I was never honest with anybody, never revealed a bit of my soul. But she seemed different, familiar. "Kidney failure. On dialysis twice a week every week since..."

Coralee tilted her head and I swear I saw a billowy sparkle in her eyes. "Since what?"

"Since I overdosed a few times. Since I destroyed my body so badly that I now have the kidneys of someone three times my age. I've been on a donor list for over a year."

A red stripe penetrated the jet back strands of her hair, which swooped over her forehead as if they were the legs of native tarantulas. She placed a hand over mine, the underside of her palm like a blanket of calming warmth. "I'm sure they'll find a donor for you soon. These bodies," she placed a finger on my chest, "were not meant to be vessels for pain."

We talked for what felt like hours, me never asking questions about her life, where she lived, or her career. I reached to the core, found myself telling Coralee about the first time I used and why, to this day, the urge is still there, like a nagging itch that can't be scratched. She listened and held my hand, not once interrupting me. An autumn moon dripped platelets of dark light upon us through the streets of the city. It could have been around midnight when she broke our stride and faced me.

"You need to get some rest, now. Boylston Station is up ahead. I'm going to head home." She kissed me on the cheek and the rumble of comfort filled my bones. Before leaving, she slipped a piece of paper into my hand. "Good night."

I waved goodbye and walked away, not once questioning the evening's intent.

#

The morning sun pinched the sides of my brain. I couldn't remember the last time I had actually slept throughout a whole night without tossing and turning, without the pinch of pain stifling my every second of slumber. My dreams were filled with clouds, with light. The small piece of paper was still sitting on my nightstand.

Harrison's Spot, Tremont Street, Friday, 7:00pm.

I peered at the alarm clock. I had slept into the afternoon. Three years of my visits to Massachusetts General Hospital for dialysis, and I couldn't help but stroll through the city for hours afterwards before heading home. It was as if I were afraid to go home, to sit in a sullen room where pain eluded pleasure and I was alone with nothing but my thoughts. I looked at my face in the bedroom mirror, noticed that my cheeks were flush with a rosy apple glow instead of their usual dull, pale. Even my eyes had a bright residue beyond the dark brown swath.

The bed beckoned me again, and within moments, I was asleep again, free to slip into another place that was far beyond the torment of the day.

#

It's not a craving. Cravings pass and do not often involve substances that could shut down an immune system. It's always there, floating behind the fibers within the brain, buried and building a nest from pieces of the past. It's at your weakest point, when you think it'll be okay for just a small taste, that it strikes and kills.

It knows no emotion, no bias. It doesn't care how long you've lived or how many children you've raised. It's there, and I know it. It'll never leave, never go away. It won't jump to another soul or eventually fade away.

It'll win. And I'll lose.

#

She was already at Harrison's Spot, a monolithic beauty with a grin that set the world ablaze. She leaned against the brick exterior of the restaurant, tight black jeans and a white sweater that revealed only the slightest bits of pale cleavage.

"Trent," she said, and stood up to greet me. The hug stopped time, aroused a static shockwave through my fingers and toes. "How are you feeling?"

My mind was already on the truth before the words could catch up. "I feel...great. For a change, at least." I could tell I was smiling.

"That's so good to hear. Come on, let's get a drink."

We sat at a table towards the back of the bar section of Harrison's. It was unusually quiet for a Friday evening, the loudest sounds of the night spun from a jukebox in the corner of the room. U2's "Angel of Harlem" radiated throughout the dewy bar.

We shared a pitcher of beer, talking about everything from my childhood (I grew up in Salem, not too far from the site of the original Witch Trials) to her upbringing in New York City (she was adopted and didn't know her biological parents). Coralee told me she had a degree in art history but spent the last year or so volunteering at animal shelters while she interviewed for professor gigs in and around the Boston area.

I was on my last glass when she eventually asked me a question I hoped she wouldn't.

"Will you ever use again?"

I couldn't face her, only peered into the bottom of my glass until the liquid was far into my body. "I don't know, Coralee. I don't."

She placed her hand over mine and there it was again. The

warmth, the comfort, the familiar, like I had known her for twenty years instead of only a day or two. "Tell me that you won't."

I bit the inside of my cheek and metallic tinges of blood slowly trickled down to my tongue. "I...won't."

Two rows of perfect white teeth and a crinkle of her freckled nose. She leaned in for a kiss and when her blood red lips touched mine a shiver of fire crisped the edges of my heart.

# #

Coralee lay by my side, nestled within the gap between my arm and chest. She smelled like lilac blossoms and winter morning snow. She kissed the edge of my chin, nuzzled her nose against the brownish red stubble on my face. I drifted in and out, watched the walls of my bedroom collapse and reveal the endless black of space and nighttime stars. I could feel the bed floating, as if we were somewhere beyond the reaches of time.

Coralee slid to the edge of the bed and stood up, the arch of onyx wings outstretched to the sky. Glints of broken moonlight danced in the forefront and I reached for her. Her wings shuttered like a blurry comet and within moments she was gone.

# #

A slow fade to white. The strike of Saturday morning forced open my eyelids. I was alone in the bedroom, bedsheets unwrinkled except for those covering my body. It took me a full minute or two before I realized that Coralee was missing. My frantic search resulted in not a trace of her presence in my apartment. I had no way to reach her, no phone number or address.

Not even a last name.

The clock on my nightstand indicated that was nearing eleven a.m. If I didn't hop on a train to Mass General within the next fifteen minutes, I would miss my dialysis appointment.

#

"Hmm."

I tilted my head in confusion. "What's wrong?"

Betty, one of the many nurses that routinely attended to my visits, read a series of numbers to herself on a monitor beyond the dialysis machine. "This isn't normal."

"What is it?"

Betty left me alone for a moment and returned with Dr. O'Connell. He didn't acknowledge me.

"Doc, what's going on? Am I okay?"

He tapped a few keys on the computer attached to the machine and shook his head. "This can't be right, Betty. Is something wrong with this device?"

"Doctor, it was serviced just a few days ago." Betty flipped through a shuffling of papers next to the monitor.

"Doc!"

He finally turned around to face. "Trent, this...sorry. Let me ask you: how do you feel?"

I told him the truth. "Fine. No pain. Feeling pretty good."

"Trent, have you taken anything? Any meds that we haven't prescribed?" His face was as inquisitive as a child's.

I shook my head. "Nope."

"Well," he began, "your values are clean. It's almost as if there's nothing wrong with your kidneys, Trent. This is unbelievable."

And all I could think of was Coralee. She disappeared in my dreams and I didn't know where to find her. Dr. O'Connell unhooked me and informed that I should come back later in the day for some tests. I jogged to the cafeteria, hoping that, just maybe, she'd be here.

But she wasn't, and I was questioning my reality.

#

I could tell you more, how I walked throughout the city for the rest of the day, from one edge of Boston to the other. I swear that I passed every bar, every goddamn coffee shop, all to no avail. The itch, it was there the entire time, poking at the edges of my mind. It broke me down, syphoned my thoughts at their weakest point.

It didn't take long to find what I needed. It finds you, it knows what you need and how much you should put inside of you.

And now I'm here, at a motel just outside of the city. She was real and she wasn't. The first hot injection into my arm told me that. A last connection of warmth, one final link to humanity before it all came to this. She may be overhead, searching for another soul to fix, scanning the darkest corners of the city.

Coralee, you're gone. And I know why you were here.

Jagged edges of dim moonlight poke through a small slit in the curtain, a frenetic waltz of incandescence and lost hope.

Acknowledgments

There is perhaps one significant attribute that I've learned about myself over the past six years as a writer: there are multiple voices inside of my head and I never know which one is going to speak when I sit down with an empty page in front of me.

The stories in Sixteen Small Deaths span a wide range of voices, from the horror of "Saffron," the emotional tinges of "December," to the neo-noir of "Midnight Souls." I believe this reflects the artistic nature of the modern writer and the poignant avenues that live deep within our souls. Or, as I've sometimes explained: I've been influenced from a multitude of sources, including Will Christopher Baer, "The Twilight Zone," Chuck Palahniuk, Craig Clevenger, Stephen King, "Tales from the Darkside," old-school zombie movies, and slasher flicks. I guess that when all is said and done, all of these influences have some representation in my work.

So, Reader, I hope you've enjoyed this collection. These stories are part of my muscle fiber, part of the gray web covering my brain. Some of these stories were written before I really knew what I was doing, and others were penned years after I finally found my voice as a writer. Some are fantastic reinforcements of the neo-noir genre, while others straddle the line between literary and genre fiction.

Readers, thanks for your time. I hope I've entertained you.

#

This collection wouldn't be possible without the tireless love, support and devotion of several key people in my life. First and foremost, I'd like to thank my beautiful wife, Sarah, for being my foundation and believing in me all of these years. I love you and couldn't be more thankful for your support. (Thanks and hugs go to my furry children, as well: Cody, Gracie, Phineas, Harper and Atticus.)

A significant chunk of thanks goes to Phil Jourdan, founder of Perfect Edge Books. Phil, thanks for believing in this collection, and thanks for all of your hard work in seeing this thing through.

A round of thanks to my family and friends: Babbo, Angela, Baby Nicky and Lisa (as well as the Gucciardi, Towne and Jacobs families). Extra special thanks to Dr. Ryan Fielding, who was often the first reader for many of these stories and provided invaluable feedback where it was needed.

To my fellow writers, thanks for being who you are: Axel Taiari, Richard Thomas, Nik Korpon, Craig Wallwork, Gordon Highland, Pablo d'Stair, Mark Grover, Andrez Bergen, Jesse Lawrence, Pela Via, Caleb Ross, Anthony Jacques, Michael Gonzalez, Jason Heim, Max Gladstone, Chris Deal, Colin McKay Miller, Craig Clevenger, Stephen Graham Jones, Will Christopher Baer, Chuck Palahniuk, Donald Ray Pollock, Drew McCoy, Edward Rathke, Gabrielle Faust, Max Barry, Chelsea Cain, Monica Drake, Nicholas Karpuk, Paul Eckert, Sean P. Ferguson, everyone at The Velvet and Write Club, as well as the fellas at Booked Podcast (Livius and Robb).

Thanks,

Christopher J. Dwyer
January 2013

**PERFECT
EDGE
BOOKS**

"There are many who dare not kill themselves for fear of what the neighbours will say," Cyril Connolly wrote, and we believe he was right.

Perfect Edge seeks books that take on the crippling fear of other people, the question of what's correct and normal, of how life works, of what art is.

Our authors disagree with each other; their styles vary as widely as their concerns. What matters is the will to create books that won't be easy to assimilate. We take risks, not for the sake of risk-taking, but for the things that might come out of it.